WHAT PEOPLE ARE SAYING

"Successful corporate executive, gifted artist, and poet Stevie Tate demonstrates that his immense creative talent also extends to writing books in *On the Ledge of Life*. At first glance, it appears to be a book about a man struggling with a terminal illness and his mortality; however, you quickly realize that it's a very moving story about love, spirituality, and the full circle of life. Through the main character's journey of discovery, the book addresses the impact of our choices on our happiness, our health, and the people around us. Readers will be hooked from the start and treated to a story that evokes every emotion, captures the imagination, and most importantly touches the heart and inspires them to live a better life.

One the Ledge of Life will be meaningful to people from all walks of life, young or old. However, it is a must-read for individuals struggling with balance in their lives or a perfect gift for them from the people who love them. It's also a great resource book for life and executive coaches looking for an excellent client tool to spark important conversations on work/life balance issues. With strong messages woven into a story format, it provides a strong catalyst for action by encouraging clients to reflect on their own choices and take steps to a more positive and fulfilling future before it's too late."

—Tricia McCreary,
CPC, Professional Coach, Thrive NOW Solutions

"*On the Ledge of Life* is an inspiring, heartfelt story of a man who, through the reality of death, comes to the realization of life. Allen, the main character, who is faced with his own mortality, goes on a long, treacherous journey in search for his truth and purpose, and he finds it in the place where it has always been and always will be—within himself. The author and story invite us to go on an exploration within ourselves and examine our own life and truths, for nothing invigorates life like the reality of death. *On the Ledge of Life* teaches us all how to truly live."

—Dr. Noah Daniel

"Stevie Tate does a sensational job of sharing with the reader his lifelong commitment to personal growth and spiritual development through a wonderfully written and touching story that opens the reader's heart and mind while seamlessly making the sometimes difficult or uncomfortable subject matter intimately personal, easy, and enjoyable to read. *On the Ledge of Life* is certain to become a classic read, as it will continue to touch generation after generation with its insights, love, and honesty about a life worth living."

—Grant Moyer,
President, Momentum Fitness Solutions

"Stevie Tate writes a disarming tale in a folksy sort of way yet is exceptionally sophisticated in his thinking process. A fascinating culmination of a man's mind, spirit, heart, and life experiences.

Full of poignant wisdom, this book needs to be on every night-stand in every language so that it can at least be seen if not read every day as a reminder of the quality of life and great happiness we are all capable of having. It is the ultimate, pure platinum self-help book of the world we now live in for all who need encouragement and change in their lives.

This book is full of prayers to be prayed daily, thoughts to carry with you daily. This book exemplifies purity, intelligence, and incredible human insight! His absolute candor and honesty will captivate you."

—Bernadette Fiaschetti,
Co-founder Pizza Patron, Co-founder
Wing Stop restaurants, Philanthropist

ON THE LEDGE OF LIFE

a novel

Stevie Tate

Tate Publishing & Enterprises

Published by Tate Publishing & Enterprises, LLC
127 E. Trade Center Terrace | Mustang, Oklahoma 73064 USA
1.888.361.9473 | www.tatepublishing.com

Tate Publishing is committed to excellence in the publishing industry. The company reflects the philosophy established by the founders, based on Psalm 68:11,
"The Lord gave the word and great was the company of those who published it."

Book design copyright © 2010 by Tate Publishing, LLC. All rights reserved.
Cover design by Blake Brasor
Interior design by Jeff Fisher

Published in the United States of America

ISBN: 978-1-61663-759-0
1. Fiction, Christian, General
2. Fiction, Visionary & Metaphysical
10.09.01

ACKNOWLEDGMENTS

To all those who touched my life in one way or another, I thank you. There have been so many conversations, so many moments of truth and reflection. My journey through this book and life could not have been possible without you. Each of you served a purpose; each one of you helped me to learn and grow and still do. I pray each day that in some way I touched you as well.

RePaula Tate. How many hours have you lent your time and ears to listen to me? I would not be the man I am today if not for you. I am eternally grateful for our friendship and our love affair.

Noah Daniels, my mentor; Tricia McCreary, my life coach; Scott Donaldson, my calm in the storm, and Grant Moyer my inspiration, words cannot describe the eternal gratitude I have for your friendship. You all know how I feel about you.

I also want to thank each of you in advance, whom I have not yet encountered. I can only imagine the conversations we will have and revelations we will have.

You, the one in front of me! You are my teacher; truth and wisdom flows from your lips like honey; may you receive the same.

Thank you, God, for being God. I love you—you are my true love affair!

INTRODUCTION

Think about the paths that each one of us are on.
When we really look at each other under the same light, we are not
that much different. Yes, our stories vary and the roads we travel
down take different turns, but our wants, needs, and desires are very
similar. We want to love and be loved, we want to feel at peace, and
we want to have a greater sense of purpose. Nobody really wants to
struggle or have drama in their lives; nobody really wants to have
hurts and pain. Yet another of the commonalties we have is that we
do very little to have what we truly want and make changes; we do
very little to become our highest selves.

I did write the book so that maybe just one person might read
it and be touched in some way. You see, if I had my wish, we would
all be completely filled with purpose, joy, and happiness. I hate to
see people hurt and struggle, including myself. I have spent most of
my life asking why we do, and I think that is why God finally said,
"Here, write this book, and you will understand why, and maybe
some of the readers will as well."

This story came to me one night as I lay awake in bed praying.
I used to be a severe insomniac and would lie in bed all night just

thinking and contemplating life. Over the next few years, I started questioning my life and all the struggles, drama, and lack of peace but continued going down the same path over and over. I would put all of my thoughts down on paper and, when I had time, try to make sense of them.

It was not until I actually started writing this book that my life started changing. At the time, I was a regional vice president for a Fortune Five Hundred company and my life was absolutely crazy. I had just gotten married for the second time, and my whole life was a job and a lifestyle. I was stressed out and anxiety ridden.

I had many destructive patterns that I just could not break and that kept me a prisoner of my own making. From the outside my life looked fantastic. I had money, success, and everything that most people only dreamed of. But day after day I struggled to make sense of the life I had created; inside, I was being eaten alive.

Long story short, I ended up in the fetal position in a hotel room a long way from home. After making my way home, my doctor told me that if I didn't make some serious changes, I would be dead in a year. Ouch. So along with a feeling that there had to be more to life than what I was experiencing, I left a storied career, which most people said was crazy, and set out to understand this life we live and find out the truth.

Well, all that sounds simple, but it wasn't. Leaving a seventeen-year lifestyle comes with a whole other set of issues. I'm not even going to attempt to go into all those. Just trust me when I say the struggle continued. Another divorce, more drama, more hurt, and things I didn't even know one could go through.

As I said, when I started writing the book, my life started to change, very slowly at first, but more and more as I put the thoughts on paper and contemplated each one. I found myself on my knees many, many times. I found myself reaching, digging deep inside. I spent a whole lot of time by myself knowing that I had an opportunity. I could either continue on just making the same mistakes and living without choice, or I could look at this period of time to change my life. I had already squandered too many opportunities in my life, and I was committed to not doing the same again.

So here you have this book, a God story, a love story, and a man's full circle of life in search for the truth of life. It's not a book about the disease the character has. The disease could be one of a thousand things we all have in our lives that are challenging us. But for whatever reason, it's the story that was revealed to me and I was told to write.

Yes, writing this book has changed my life in many ways, and if that's all that ever comes from it, then it served a greater purpose. I no longer suffer from all the madness I once did. Life, as it pertains to the way I live it, does make much more sense to me, and I know what is important: my soul and my spirit. I have peace in my life now, and I see the possibilities of becoming my highest self.

My hopes and prayers are that those of you who read this story will start to ask yourself some of the same questions I did. What is the truth about my life, and how do I correct it before it's too late?

I love each of you. I know that statement is hard to understand, but it is how I feel. I know your struggles and your hurts and your dramas. I know the things that consume your thoughts. There is very little that you have gone through or are going through that I have not experienced. But know this: you can let go of the past; you can start over. You can make changes that will change your life and the lives of others, and you can live an incredible, magical, abundant life.

One last thought before you move on.

What are you waiting for?

Free your mind of doubt, fear, hurt, and disbelief.

Know what you know is the real truth, that those feelings are not real. They are illusions created by sensory memories that you have stored and now use as a reference to calculate and justify your existence in what you think is reality.

The only truth is what you have determined is the truth. This can be changed anytime and anywhere. Your mind is an accumulation of thoughts to serve you only as a protective mechanism. Its operation is to keep you from making decisions that might cease your life. Your mind is programmed with this so that you won't jump off a cliff believing you can fly. But can you?

Nothing exists unless you decide or believe it does. Not fear, not stress, not anxiety, and not hurt. Don't rely on your self-preserving mind to make those decisions, or you will continue to live within the context of those limitations.

Your mind is not hiding the truth; it does not know how to. It is only you living in your mind. Escape your mind and you will see the possibilities that are unimaginable and without limitations. Separate yourself from your mind to see the truth ... and who you really are.

LISA, LIFE, AND THE DOCTOR

Monday morning.

The air was crisp and clean, and all was right with my world. It was one of those days when you could actually feel life all around you. The birds were singing their respective arias, the sun was bright and comforting, and the essence of flowers lingered in the air. I couldn't help but smile from the sheer joy of being alive.

If only every day of my life could be like that. But days like that seem to have become extremely elusive. With maturity comes responsibility, and with responsibility comes stress and issues. Exit days of sheer joy, sunshine, arias, and floral scents. At that moment I wondered what it would be like to have this feeling every day. To be in that mystical thing they call the flow of life. To live without the struggles, fear, the drama, the constant questioning, the feeling that you just can't get it right.

What would it be like?

"What's for dinner tonight?" I asked Lisa, my wife, leaving my reverie behind.

"We'll figure something out. What sounds good?"

"Anything you make or order will be fine with me." I left through the door to the garage.

I got behind the wheel, put my Ford Explorer in reverse, and smiled as I pulled out of the drive. The radio was turned on with the Rolling Stones cranked up, and the wind was blowing through my hair. Life felt good today, like it should. I felt like a champion, like I was on fire.

I made my way down the usual route, which is about a forty-two-minute trip, not that I clocked it or anything. I had been making the same trip for five years, three months, and a few days. That particular Monday, however, something was different. I couldn't put my finger on it, but something was definitely not the same. It wasn't just that I felt good emotionally for once, but more like something had changed or was changing in my life. I made the usual left turn into the gate at Corporate Hamster Cage, showed my ID, and hoped to dive the Explorer into the closest parking space. As usual, the nearest parking space was floors away from where I began the insanity. *Someday,* I thought, *I'll start out earlier and arrive earlier. Why create more stress than I already have?*

Once I got inside the building and headed for my office, more stress started setting in—that dreaded feeling, the anxiety, fear, and uncertainty. The euphoria I had been experiencing earlier was quickly evaporating and feeling miles behind.

You would think after five years I would have mastered anything they could throw my way, but the world never sleeps, and technology is growing faster than we can learn it. The demands of just keeping up with what's new can be daunting and intimidating. There were countless e-mails that demanded responses, conference calls that lasted for hours that only created more work, and more tasks than I could ever accomplish even if there were two of me. I know

I'm not the only one who felt this way. Half of the conversations I had with my colleagues were about the same issues. I could see it in their eyes halfway through the day—part panic, part fear, part longing just to be free. Like robots performing duties for their makers, we continued. We continued with no heart and no passion. For the most part, both of those have been taken out of the workplace and replaced with tasks and initiatives. At this time, it was the bed I had made, and, barring a lottery win, it would be my own bed to lie in for a long, long time. Some days my desire to leave it all behind was so acute it nearly took my breath away.

It was not just the lack of heart at the workplace that left me empty; it was the void and lack of hunger in the rest of my life as well. It was the low expectations I had of myself, the halfhearted living. I wanted more, much more. I wanted a big, glorious, powerful life filled with desire and passion. But there was just so much stuff that seemed to get in the way of pursuing those feelings at any length.

Throughout the rest of that day, through the meetings, phone calls, rushing faster, and getting it all done, in the back of my mind there was a troublesome feeling, that feeling that something was different; something was about to happen. I couldn't explain it, nor did I know what it was. It was just a feeling, an awareness. Something was happening, or was it?

Up to this point, my life was about the same as that of most other people, where everything appeared to be one big corporation, kind of like that movie *The Matrix*. I would do my best to get through each day and try to make sense out of everything, or even something. For me, that was a full-time task. In fact, most of my life I'd been trying to figure out this thing we call life. I'd had my share of successes and failures, my share of depression and joy, my share of struggles and dramas. But there always seemed to be something missing, a void inside, something that I needed to know, something I needed to feel and didn't. I yearned for it; I prayed for it; I waited for it.

Like most people, I gave some effort to life. I would exercise a little and every now and then eat healthy. I read books that promised the answer to life and some Sundays even went to church. I would get excited about the plans that I would make for my life and spend time putting together the chart to execute them. But complacency, laziness, and the lack of discipline always got the best of me. Day after day frustration from lack of progress would haunt me. So to escape the fact that I wasn't really getting anywhere in life, I would escape into the TV, drink too much, work too much, and then spend the rest of my time worrying and stressing about everything else.

For the most part, I felt I was fairly well adjusted. I had what I believed was a relationship with God, although even after all the books I'd read I was still not on any certain path. Certain questions had plagued me, haunted me, most of my adult life. *What is the truth of life? How will I ever know what it is? How will I find it?*

I had good friends and people around me who loved me, and I had a little money saved. But like most, I struggled every day trying to figure out something I couldn't explain. *What is my destiny? What is my purpose? How can I live a happier life, and how do I make sense of all the madness and drama? How do I end all the struggles?*

I looked into the eyes of my associates at work and people I met on the street. It was as if I was looking into the soulless eyes of automatons, moving, doing, performing without passion or thought. I looked into the eyes of their discontent and saw myself reflected back. Each of us was dealing with many of the same problems and issues—relationships, money, unhealthy diets, too much drama, job issues, time constraints, lack of direction, lack of peace, the inability to change. How many of us move through life without any real purpose, without direction? It's as if we are always waiting. Something is coming. Something will happen to make it all meaningful. One day each of us will wake up and care again, be young at heart again, believe in life again. But until then, we keep waiting and wondering what that will be ... and when. We watch time pass us by, every day thinking that someday something will just magically happen to change our reality, our existence. Something will happen that will make us change. Like a date on a calendar, we search, we long for, and we wait.

Lisa and have been married for six years. We married after just three months of dating. We didn't want to wait. We could not wait. We were madly in love and sure there was no one else for either of us. We had so much passion for each other, and we respected one another. For the first time in my life, I was able to genuinely care about another person in every way. We were the couple that defined words like love and soul mates. Friends, family, even total strangers would bask in the glow of what we had, wishing they could have what we shared. The wonderment of fresh, clean, pure, unadulterated love draws people in and allows them to dream along with you. Every time someone commented on the awesomeness of our unity, I would look at my beautiful Lisa and swell with pride. My desire for her was ceaseless. She was captivating, and she loved only me.

Lisa, on any scale, is a breathtaking beauty and so much more. She's a statuesque blonde of five feet, eight inches, with a body perfectly proportioned to entice and excite the libido of any man. Her smile is the most beautiful smile God has ever created and put on the face of a woman. Her eyes draw me in and cause certain headiness, intoxication greater than any mortal-made wine. She knew what she did to me, and she languished in the knowledge that I was so into her. All of those things are the earthy, human part of Lisa. She also has a soul of beauty that surpasses anyone I had ever known. There is a great spirit about her. No matter whom she met or where, she made a friend. The perfect hostess, the perfect companion, the perfect date, she is everything I could have asked for if I had written a list of what I wanted in a wife. And she was spontaneous, not just in our love life but in everything.

We used to love taking long road trips without direction, always taking the back roads to add to the adventure. We would get excited along the way, wondering what great little hole-in-the-wall restaurants we would find, and a time or two had too many margaritas and would have to find the nearest hotel before continuing on. Silly movies use lines like *she completes me,* but in our case it was so true. Everything I was not, Lisa was. Most of all, she believed in me, loved me, and I always felt I had done nothing to deserve the completeness of this woman.

Our first years together were pure pleasure. We did everything together in our free time. We had long conversations and talked about out future in detail. Our evenings were about cooking together and long walks. Then as it happens, little things that had started to accumulate added up, and before we knew it they had become the center of what used to be our incredible conversations. Day by day everything just seemed to become so complicated. It was like a web was being spun and we were headed right for it. Though there were still some good days and great moments, they were short lived.

Like many marriages, we lost our focus and forgot how important we were to one another. Words were said, things were done that overshadowed all the beauty we once had, and that basket of the past issues filled up. The ability to communicate just seemed to vanish, and the connection we once had vanished. Time just seemed to be our enemy.

Each and every day brought more issues for us to struggle over. We still went through the motions, living like everything was all right, and we tried to the extent that we could. The love was still there, but all of the things that make a relationship work—like communication, trust, friendship, and taking time for each other—seemed to be all but forgotten. From that point, there just seemed to be so much confusion and blame that filled our conversations, disconnection! We were just tired of talking about it. It felt many times like we were just like a ticking time bomb, but neither of us was ready to light the fuse, or had we already? I knew things were wrong, but I was too close, too involved to know how to fix them.

Our issues had become a part of the day-to-day stresses. Our blame and finger pointing became part of the deception. How could I love her so much but not seem to be able to fix our problems? How I had flirted with the romantic thought of being out of this situation only to be horrified of being alone and without the only thing that meant anything to me.

So as I often do, I took out my pen and pad and began to write what was on my mind and my heart. I don't know if any of these things I write make since or not, but they are what feel and what I'm inspired to write. I can only imagine what someone will think if they ever find these.

> She believes I would be better off without her:
> Is the bird better off without the sky?
> Is the river better off without the mountains?
> Is the dark better off without the light?
> Is sugar better off without salt?
> Is hot better off without cold?
> Is good better off without evil?
> Is happiness better off without hurt?
> Is God better off without the devil?
> Is life better off without death?
> She believes time will make things right.
> I just don't know.
> I love you, Lisa.
> Allen

As with most days, I still had all the same challenges and struggles. I would put in a twelve-hour day dealing with problems that I did and didn't create, and as usual, by the end of the day I was drained. The unresolved issues between Lisa and I were still there to deal with when I got home, but I hoped she would be tired too and we wouldn't have to plunge into them. There were family issues to resolve, bills to pay, the need to catch up with a buddy, and somehow get in a workout before bedtime, which I would probably skip. My day just ended abruptly, kind of like a car crash, like many before it.

As I awoke Tuesday, the tranquility of Monday's start quickly gave way to the normal routine. I hurried around trying to find the keys, my wallet, phones, and all the other things it takes to get me through the day. Thus the stress began. Raining down on me like a waterfall, the tension began building with my morning shower. *How,* I asked myself, *can getting up and getting ready for the day cause so much anxiety? My mind races constantly with all that hasn't even happened yet. Good REM sleep seems to be out of my grasp. This has got to stop; it's got to change!*

But like always, I somehow pulled it together and made my way out the door. As I walked into the garage, a very sharp pain went right up the middle of my abdominal area. It was like I had swallowed a burning coal. I didn't know whether to scream or cry. The pain was sharp and deep, leaving me weak and shaking. And then it left about as fast as it had come, so I said nothing to Lisa. It was probably just my body reacting to my lifestyle. Back on the road and off to another day at the office. I thought this could be the day I'd get lucky and find a good parking space. I was, after all, running a whole two minutes ahead of schedule. Hope was rising. Maybe this day would be different.

As I turned right on Frankford Street, the pain hit me again. This time it felt more like a Mack truck had crashed into me. I couldn't breathe. I couldn't think. Like before, it burned, cramped, twisted. It took what felt like hours for the pain to subside. My body was soaked in sweat, and my heart was pounding like a drum. I tried to focus on driving. I tried to relax my mind. I tried to take deep breaths, but the pain was too intense. *Surely this cannot be a heart attack,* my mind screamed. *I'm too young!*

This felt different, not like what I had heard a heart attack should feel like. Something told me this pain was more than just something I had eaten, and I was scared. Not one to run to the doctor for every scrape and bruise, I made the decision to drive directly to the office of my physician, Dr. Moyer. I wasn't sure why, but I was certain this pain signified something very serious.

The drive to the doctor's office was a short one, no more than five miles from where I was driving at the time of the attack. The office was in one of those neighborhoods where, for some reason, those who lived there before sold their beautiful homes to other people who opened up businesses. You know the ones I'm talking about. Great little neighborhoods in quaint little areas where the houses are older with big majestic trees and perfectly manicured lawns. Now there was a dentist office and a Farmer's Insurance, a small art gallery, and, of course, a doctor's office. Dr. Moyer had been my doctor for years, although I rarely had need of his services except for flu, and once a case of athlete's foot. I liked the fact that he knew me by my first name and would give me a little more attention than first-time patients.

"Good morning, Allen, how are you? What's wrong? Got the flu? Athlete's foot again? Or have you created a new malady for me?" Dr. Moyer said with a smile.

Doctor humor must be taught in medical school and be a very funny inside joke for doctors only. They seem to find it comforting to entertain their patients with some not-so-funny humorous remarks. It's probably meant to be a good ice-breaker and opens the door for the patient to begin his or her tale of all their health issues. But right now I was a little unnerved and not to jovial.

"Well, whatever the case, I'm sure we can fix you up. How's that beautiful wife?"

Like most times, I was a little embarrassed to be sitting there when it was probably some trivial problem like bad indigestion, but I wouldn't admit that to the doc. So I responded with cheer.

"Great; in fact life is good. No major news on the home front." But that was not really the truth. I couldn't come out and tell Dr. Moyer my life was in shambles and my marriage was crumbling. He gave me that look that told me he could see right through my lies but knew better than to push; besides, he was not a psychiatrist.

"Well, good; jump up here on the table, and tell me why you're here."

"Probably nothing, but this morning at the house and then again on the way to work, I had these really bad pains in my midsection, kind of right in the middle. I just about passed out because the pain was so bad."

Just like always, he brought out the stethoscope and started listening to my chest and abdomen. That's another thing I never understood. If you tell the doctor your foot hurts, he takes out that cold piece of metal and listens to your heart.

"Well, no wonder you had a pain. You have this loud beating in your chest," he joked. More humor.

"Doc, I don't mean to sound unappreciative, but I really do need to get to the office," I said more irritably than I meant. This wasn't his fault.

"Maybe that's why you have the pain, always rushing to get somewhere else. Relax for a minute, and let me take a look at you."

For the next several minutes, he poked and he prodded; he palpated and listened; he listened and looked all serious and officious. After a while, he spoke.

"I'm going to ask Janet to come in and get a blood sample; then I want you to leave me a little present in this cup."

"Sure, Doc. What do you think it could be? I have been under a lot of stress lately," I said with some fear.

"I don't know yet, but I think we need to find out," he said reassuringly, patting my arm as he said it.

As I waited for the results, I did get to read a good story on how Canadian geese manage to fly all the way from Canada to Mexico every year to breed. I wondered what he was going to tell me. Would it be something I already knew, like I needed to eat healthier, get more rest, and reduce the amount of stress? If that was all it was, he'd probably give me some of those freebie pills and say he wanted to see me back here in two weeks. That would have been just fine with me.

As time ticked on, my mind started wandering, flitting from one thing to another. *What's taking them so long? I probably should call the office. I'll tell Lisa about this tonight. I need to call the plumber. Lisa's parents are coming in this weekend. I need to save more money. I bet the good doctor makes some cash. How can I change my life? I should go to church more. I wonder if I will ever win the lottery. I need to start running more. Does Lisa still want me? Do I still want her? Will I hit my bonus this year? I wonder how my sisters are doing. I need to get more organized. God, what if there is something seriously wrong with me?* On and on my mind raced.

This was ridiculous. I was becoming impatient. I could no longer concentrate on reading and was becoming very fidgety. Nearly an hour had gone by, and that was about the extent of my patience. The pain had subsided to a large degree, and I was now feeling silly for being there and sure it was nothing serious. I realized that old sawbones didn't have the best equipment in town and that I didn't have an appointment, but I was late for work. I needed to get a move on, and there was so much I needed to do. I thought I'd better call the office and let them know how late I would be.

Once again stress and worry filled my mind; just a few hours lost would put me behind. It seemed as if one little thing out of the ordinary got in my way, it threw the whole day into a tailspin, then the week, the month, and the year.

At long last, Dr. Moyer made his way in, a stack of papers in his hands and his glasses down at the end of his nose.

"Doc, where have you been? I'm already late for work and need to get going. Do you want me to come back later?"

"Sorry for the wait," Dr. Moyer said. "I will call you later today when I get more information, if I find anything."

It's funny how sometimes in life you feel like you know what's going to happen before it actually does. Not that you actually know what is going to happen but like something or someone is whispering in your ear, giving you an indication. By the look in Dr. Moyer's face, I knew I was getting ready to hear something that wasn't good.

Later that day while in the office, I tried to concentrate on my work, but my mind just kept thinking about the look in Dr. Moyer's eyes. Everything was murky-like, and it was like I really wasn't there. I heard the voices around me. I looked into the computer screen, but nothing registered in my brain. It was that same feeling you get when you are really nervous, like your brain dumps some kind of endorphin in your body that makes you feel like you're in a dream.

When the call finally came, I was totally absorbed in a foggy state of mind and jumped at the ringing of the phone.

"Allen, this is Dr. Moyer. I would like you to check into the hospital for a few tests. Your lab results are showing something, but I'm going to need some more tests before we know anything more. When can I meet you at Baylor hospital?"

"You mean right away? Like today?" I was stunned by his words.

"I don't think this is something we should wait on, Allen. Let's not take any chances. Can you check in this evening? I'll make rounds about six or six thirty and check on you then. And Allen, don't worry; it might be nothing. I just want to reassure both of us."

With those few words, he was gone. I wished I'd asked him how long I'd be away from work or what I should tell Lisa, but I didn't want to call him back. Instead, I put everything back into my briefcase, told the secretary I had to hurry to an appointment, and left the office.

On my way to the car, the only words reverberating through my throbbing head were Dr. Moyers, *I don't think this is something we should wait on; let's not take any chances.* All the bravado went out of me, and I wanted to be held, to be reassured that everything was okay and I wasn't really sick. I needed Lisa. I needed her to hold me and tell me she still loved me and that we were together forever. I needed Lisa to pack a bag and run away with me and leave this crazy life behind.

I was so scared. How could this be happening? Not knowing what the future had in store for me was the worst. Thinking about all the possible outcomes, it was hard to find any relief or comfort. It was almost impossible to concentrate and focus on what to do next.

I remember when Lisa and I used to have those long, deep conversations back before careers and mortgages. I always told her if I ever was diagnosed with a terminal disease, she should just let me die at home, or, if I could, I would want to die in peace somewhere in the mountains far away from the humiliation of probing doctors and friends dropping by to see how bad I looked.

I had seen what had happened to my best friend, Doug. He was diagnosed with cancer that attacked and consumed his body like a school of piranhas. In just a matter of two months, a perfectly healthy and totally athletic, beautiful person was reduced to the shell of the man he had been. It was a horrific death. I will never forget how, when we were alone, he begged me to shut down the machines and just let him die.

"Allen, if you care about me in the least, you will not let me die like this," Doug would cry. I laid awake in my bed those last weeks of his life, thinking about the things I had told Lisa in past conversations about how I would never die like that.

Many people say things like that without ever believing it will actually happen to them. In most cases, it's a way for a man to show how tough he is, how he is not afraid of death. Some of that was true for me as well, but more than anything, to die the kind of death that Doug did scared me beyond belief. I just couldn't imagine that being the end for me.

For one solid month before Doug passed, I thought of nothing but that. If I pulled the plug as Doug asked, then I could be put in prison for murder. If I didn't, I would watch someone who was as close to me as a brother die an agonizing, pitiful death. How could I live with either decision? Would he come back to haunt me for the one thing I couldn't do? It was then and there that I decided that if I was ever put in that position, the position Doug was in, I wouldn't tell anyone. I would just take off, never to be seen again. I couldn't imagine asking someone else to end my life knowing what the consequences for them would be. And I would not put myself in the situation of having someone else in control of my last days.

Driving home, the pain returned and I cried. People in other cars would stare at me at stoplights, but I didn't care. On any other normal day I would be on the phone or thinking about many of life's issues, but that day I was in pain and afraid, and it didn't really matter what anyone thought. Lisa wasn't home when I got there. I tried to reach her at her office but was told she was in a meeting. No chance she'd pick up her cell phone then either. A short note telling her where I was and that I'd call later with more information was left on the counter in the kitchen. I just didn't know what else to say, but God, I wished she was here now.

I checked into the hospital around 4:30 p.m., went through all the motions with admissions about insurance and next of kin, and got my cute little plastic *bling* on my left wrist. Nothing felt real. I was going through all the motions, but I didn't know why. At this point, I was feeling fairly normal and stupid for checking into the hospital for something as benign as a gas pain or muscle spasm. As soon as I was in my room, a private room, I changed into the silly looking gown of medical couture and felt nearly naked.

It seemed an eternity before anyone came to check on me. When the nurse finally popped in with a cheery greeting, she took all my vitals and asked me to fill a little cup, took some more blood, and then was preparing to leave. I asked if I could have a soda, some juice, a snack of some kind—anything would do. Lunch had been something that totally slipped my mind, and now I was feeling hungry. She advised me that I would be having some tests in the morning and was not allowed to eat anything until after the tests. I decided I had been asked to check into the hospital so I could die of starvation, and I was not pleased with the arrangements.

Lisa finally called around five forty-five when she got home from work. She was hysterical, and I did everything I could to calm her, but she was already in the car rushing to the hospital. I was tempted to ask her to bring me some food, but all I requested were some decent pajamas, a good book, and her. By the time she got to the hospital, Dr. Moyer was making rounds and was standing at the end of my bed trying to be cheerful and reassuring. He was very glad to see Lisa, but then everyone always was. Her smile and demeanor could be beautiful and a bright spot in anyone's day. He explained to her that the pains I had been experiencing could be a sign of something going on, that my white blood count was a bit high, and he felt like it deserved checking out further. Plus, he felt I needed a rest, and he was so right on there.

Predictably, Lisa asked the nurse for an extra blanket and a pillow. She was going to spend the night in the chair. She even called her office and canceled all of her own appointments for the following day. I wasn't sure if she was doing this out of duty as my wife or genuine love. I hoped it was the latter. Facing the unknown while waiting on the doctor's call that day had made me realize how important certain things were to my life. The most important was Lisa. I wanted to find the right words to tell her this, but our communication wall had been built up too high, and I didn't know where to begin. Too many things were left unsaid in that time when I could have said so much, when I should have said so much. As before, I put the words down on paper as if I was documenting a sequence of events of my soul. Or maybe it was just a way for me to say the things I couldn't say out loud.

Pretend Love

You see me, I see you.

When I open the door, and when I close it

I look forward to meeting again

But forget after dinner why

If you had one wish, would it include me?

If I had one wish, it is not clear

So many face and conversations that muddy the waters

I never heard a harp

Bust something close

Is it wrong to want to the stars to fall upon me

And the love to be more powerful than me.

Wednesday morning, with Lisa at my side, I was wheeled down to the test site, or whatever it's called. I was poked, prodded, stuck, and pushed through every imaging tunnel available before being wheeled back to my room too tired to eat. After a couple of hours' sleep, orderlies came for me again and took me back for more tests—more poking, prodding, questions, bodily waste samples, and more. I can't even remember everything they did. When they were finally through with me, I was wheeled back to my room and allowed to eat a snack and drink some juice while I waited for dinner. Lisa and I shared my dinner, which consisted of things we couldn't name other than by their color. At seven when Dr. Moyer came in, he closed the door behind him and pulled up a chair. In his lap sat a large folder, my folder, holding the results of my tests and my fate. It wasn't his style to beat around the bush, so he dove straight in.

"Allen, there's a mass on your liver. All the tests indicate cancer, but I'd like to do a biopsy to make sure. The mass is rather large, so I doubt we can save the liver, but I've taken the liberty of calling Dr. Donaldson, an oncology specialist. He'll be stopping by sometime tomorrow afternoon to go over all your options, schedule the biopsy, and if it is cancer, he'll be the one to determine the treatment methods and get you on the transplant list immediately."

He looked down at his hands before addressing me again. "If there was any way I could have gotten out of telling you this news, by God, I would have. Allen, Lisa, I'm sorry. I wish I could have brought good news, but this is the best I've got today. Remember, cancer is no longer a death sentence. We have miraculous treatments available to help you get through this. It's going to be tough, but you can do it. I'll keep you both in my prayers."

He left, and the room was silent. I couldn't look at Lisa. I was a condemned man. The only thing I could do was remember Doug. He had suffered immeasurably and died a humiliating death. His family had been torn to the limits of their ability to endure as they watched him die that way. Once again I vowed not to do that to Lisa or my family. I wondered how things would be if Doug was alive and healthy. Would he help me die, or would he do as I had done?

My mind was reeling thinking of all that was getting ready to happen. I could see me lying there hooked up to the machines like Doug. I could see all my friends and family coming to see me with that look in their eyes, and then right before I allowed myself to see my funeral, it was if my mind just went blank. I didn't feel anything, I couldn't think, and it was as if time just stopped. I just lay there in a state of unconscious suspension. I could hear Lisa in the background trying her best to be positive and talk about other things, but it was like a hazy dream state. I thought about my three sisters and friends and how I would tell them. I thought about the cancer my mother had battled and all she had gone through. I didn't sleep that night. I just lay there in holding.

The next day I found myself getting probed and prodded once again, with Lisa in tow, by the specialist that Dr. Moyer put me in contact with. Dr. Donaldson was the best around I was told. He was quick and deliberate about everything he did. As I waited in between tests and probes, CT scans and MRIs, I looked around the waiting room at the other people, assuming they were there for the same reasons as I. All had the same look, like ghosts, not sure if they were still alive or already dead. They stared with blank looks out the windows and down at the floor. No one said a word to each other. I can only believe that some of us were in for the same kind of death Doug died from, and I hated thinking about it. What were they thinking of? What would the rest of their days be like? Were they ready? Are any of us?

The events followed just like the doc had said—more tests, biopsy, waiting. Lisa ran home to take care of a few things and change clothes. Being without her for those few hours was hard. Even with the problems we were having, I needed her and relied on her strength.

I was lying on the bed when Dr. Donaldson came into my room with kind of a blank look in his eyes and laid all of it on the table. It was kind of nonemotional, just a delivery of the facts. *Where is all that doctor humor now?* I remember thinking. What do you do at a time like this? The news was as bad as it could be. I had liver cancer—a large mass, inoperable, treatable, but not curable—and not a lot of time left. The liver was a major, can't-live-without-it organ. Inoperable, treatable, but not curable meant I was going to die. The final words *not much time left* sealed the deal, sealed my fate. My life was about to be over, and the world would go on without me. How much of a mark had I left on the world? I had no legacy to leave.

Dr. Donaldson finally left my room, and I dressed and left the hospital without telling anyone. The walk to my car felt like a mile; nothing looked or felt the same. Once in the car, tears started flowing. *How will I tell Lisa?* As I sat there shaking uncontrollably, the memories of Doug and what had happened to him and his last days filled my mind. I thought about the conversations I had with Lisa about this very moment, that I would never die like Doug had, and how strongly I felt about what I had said, how easy I felt the decision would be to make then. Now that I had to face the reality and make that decision, I wasn't so sure what to do.

My life was falling apart. I felt like it was crumbling down around me. My marriage was in trouble. I had no purpose, no clarity, and was far from at peace. I hadn't really accomplished anything in my life of significance, and now I'd been told I had cancer. My life, life as I had always known it, was over. How could I have cancer? That wasn't supposed to happen to me. Doesn't it always happen to someone else? I started freaking out, beating the steering wheel, crying, screaming, stomping the floor of the car.

On the way home, I stopped in at a local restaurant by the house for a drink and to just think about everything that had happened in the last seventy-two hours. How and when would I tell Lisa? What would I do about the cancer? Which of the options of treatment would I elect? The way I felt at that moment, I just wished it would have killed me without me ever knowing what happened. I was so confused, and before I knew it, I had put down four Scotch and sodas. Scotch is not good for the liver, by the way. Maybe I was punishing my body, my liver specifically, for having betrayed me.

To stave off the pain for Lisa, I told her the tests had been inconclusive and it would be a few more days before the results came back. I wanted time with her that was not marred by the black flag of cancer and death. That night, as I looked across the table at her, my thoughts raced. *This is the woman I fell in love with; this is the woman I would like to spend the rest of my life with, what little I might have left.*

How will we deal with this? I also thought about Doug. What he told me while he was dying, how he died. I thought about what I had told Lisa I would do if something like that ever happened to me. Could I really do that? *Would* I really do that?

Later that night I sat with Lisa and looked her in the eyes and told her how sorry I was for behaving and acting like I had. I told her everything that was on my mind and heart. I told her that she was the love of my life and that she was the most important thing in the world to me. I let her know how proud I was of her and how I wished I had told her that more often. I reminded her of all the conversations we used to have about life and how we would hold each other for hours staring into each other's eyes. How we would take baths together and make passionate love.

She broke down crying and held me with a fierce need to hold on, and she too apologized for being selfish and prideful. I could see and feel how much she loved me. That night we stayed up all night making love. I ran my fingers through her hair and touched every part of her body, committing it to memory. I gently kissed her hands in submission and surrendered my pride and ego.

The next morning I called work to let them know I would not be coming in that day. Of course, they asked if everything was all right. If only they knew. I spent the rest of the day walking around the house from room to room, not knowing what to do. I took a drive, but that didn't help either. On the way back, I stopped at the cemetery where Doug was buried. I sat there for hours thinking about all of our conversations. I remembered the pain and humiliation that he had gone through. I remembered the day he had pulled me close in and whispered to me, looking me straight in the eye. *"Allen, don't ever die like this. Do whatever you have to."*

THE DECISION, THE DRIVE

I knew then that the decision had already been made. Maybe it was the very moment I had said it a long time ago. Maybe I didn't have anything to do with the decision at all; maybe it was my fate. Within hours, my SUV was full of the latest and greatest camping gear from the local sporting goods store. I was amazed at how far camping gear had come in the years I'd been away in the corporate jungle. Even at a time like that I had to admit it was fun going from aisle to aisle filling the shopping cart with all the new gadgetry. I probably wouldn't need half of the stuff I selected, but what the hell? I was dying and going to the mountains to do it. Though I didn't really have a clear plan, for once in my life it didn't feel necessary. I didn't feel the need to have everything figured out and on a to-do list.

As I drove down the road, it really started to hit me. I was really dying, or was I? Was I really going to spend my last days without my wife and family? Would I really be able to leave everything and go to the mountains to die? How could I do it? I ordered my mind to think straight. I began to ask myself to give deep thought to what I was doing. Was I being rational? Was I being delusional? Was this really what I wanted, the way I wanted to leave this incarnation on earth?

It's amazing how you can be so sure of something one moment when faced with a decision and then feel like you don't know anything at all the next. I had felt so sure that when I made the statement I would go to the mountains to die, it was what I really wanted. When making the statement, I really never believed I would be forced into the position of having to back it up.

I was certain I did not want to end up like Doug. I did not want to end up dying a horrible death, withering away in some hospital room, hooked up to machines, doped up on morphine. I also did not want to have my friends looking at me with sorrow, pain, and pity in their eyes. I wanted to spend my last days looking at beauty and looking back at my life. I wanted to know the moment when I passed from this life to the next. I wanted to get as close to God as I could. I wanted to get right with God. I wanted to be at peace. I wanted to find the answers to all the questions I had been asking all my life.

Now that the decision was made, I just had to figure out how I was going to tell my wife and family that I was leaving them forever, that I was dying of cancer and going to live out my last days in the mountains. One thing that I never figured into the equation was how I would say it. *Hi, honey, I'm home; by the way, I'm dying, and I'm leaving. I'll be on a mountain somewhere contemplating the meaning of life if you need me.* How would my family take it? How would this change their lives? The fact remained, it was my life, and I should be able to decide how and where I would die. I know some people will see this as a selfish act, but until you are faced with the reality that you're dying, I don't think anyone can understand the decisions you make. In fact, I don't think I understand.

This would be the last major decision I would ever have to make.

There would be no more stress at the job, no more struggle with a crumbling marriage, no more wondering about the future, no more confusing days, no more anything. I was going to die, and once I spoke these words and accepted them, a kind of calm came over me along with that same euphoria I had felt on Monday. Monday! Subconsciously I had known this was coming, and I knew in that instant that I was making the right decision. I knew in my heart it was the only thing I could do. The rest would fall into place as time went on. I knew also the fire-of-life feeling I had felt on Monday had been in preparation for this, this one moment which defined my life and now my death. Like most of the people I know, I had spent most of my life trying to define the world around me to help me understand my life. Now I was being forced, or invited, to define who I was in relation to the world.

There were a few minor details to tend to before I could actually leave. I made out a will leaving everything to Lisa. I transferred everything from my personal savings and checking accounts to our joint account and packed a few clothes. Then I wrote Lisa a letter:

> My beautiful baby, by the time you read this letter I will be miles down the road on my way to face my destiny. Our last night together will be the very nourishment that will sustain me in the days to come. The words we shared and the truth we revealed was incredible and awe-inspiring. I don't know what will happen to me or where exactly I am going, but there is something calling me, guiding me, and lighting a path for me. Something greater than me is at work here, and for once in my life I am choosing to be in the flow of the moment and life. I know that although this will be very hard for you, you will support me in my verdict and choose to understand this decision.
>
> I have much soul searching to do and much to contemplate about this life. Though I have tried to live the best life I could, I know I could have made better decisions, loved more, and

found more joy in life. I hope and pray that during these days to come I will find the answers to questions I have been asking all my life. I hope I will be delivered the truth!

Know that you will be with me on this journey as you always have. Listen closely in your quiet moments, for I will be talking to you and thinking about you.

Wipe the tears from your eyes and smile at the opportunity that I have been given, an opportunity that I cannot deny. Let this not be one of our darkest moments but brightest. I love and adore you, and if possible, I look forward to seeing you again.

When you think of me, see me on top of the highest peaks, peering out into the world, and know I will be in the moment that was created for me.

In love and light,

Allen

The warm air from the open window was blowing on my face, and I actually felt a smile come upon my lips. I thought about how Lisa always hated the fact that even in the summer I would have the window down and the air conditioner on high. She said it hurt her ears, and there was a time or two that I let it ruin our time together by not rolling the window up. How could I have been so inconsiderate and selfish? I wish I would have just rolled it up. Man, some of the stupid things I had done because of pride and ego.

It's like I could never get what I felt in my heart to be the same in my mind and then show it through my actions. I never really wanted to act the way I did, and usually I knew what I was doing was not what I really wanted to do. It was always like a big mystery to me, one I could never figure out. None of that mattered anymore, and I would never have a chance to do things differently. I could only hope that in the days to come I would able to deal with the regret and find peace.

Straight ahead was I-35, the start of my trip to Colorado and my final days. At four thirty, the traffic in Dallas can get pretty ugly, and I could see as I pulled onto the on ramp that this day was no different. No one knew I was running away from my life, going away to die. Inching down the freeway, I looked around and wondered about all the people, wondering if some of them were going through situations like mine. There are so many people having to face different types of devastation, loss of loved ones, divorces, war, catastrophic health issues. What decisions would they make? How would they live the rest of their time? And then I thought about all the people who are just busy thinking about dinner and mowing the lawn and soccer practice, oblivious to the other side of life. I envied them.

It's probably pretty common when you're at the point I was at to feel envious of everybody else. They didn't know how good they had it. They had options, choices, and a future to think about. I would rather have had all of life's petty problems than the reality of what I was going through. It's so hard to understand why things happen as they do, and it is impossible to comprehend your own death. It's very painful to make sense of it all.

Speaking of pain, I hadn't thought about what I was going to do about the pain. That was something I hadn't considered. How bad would it get? What would it feel like? I knew in the end even the morphine didn't help Doug.

As I made my way up through Oklahoma, again I thought about how I would tell the people in my life what I was doing and why. Oh my God, what would they think? How would I get word to them? What would they think of me? What would my family do? How would they make it without me?

Most of the drive was just a blur. Seventy-two miles to Wichita, Kansas, and I realized I hadn't even looked at the map. I couldn't believe it. I had just driven 365 miles without even stopping to use the restroom, and I was very low on gas.

I looked at my dashboard clock and noticed it was eight thirty. I was sure by now Lisa had read the letter and was an absolute mess. I could see her crying, lying in the fetal position on the bed. I just couldn't think about it or I would drive myself even crazier. I was still going to have to make a call to her, but what would I say? How would I say it? I knew she would be devastated and it would be a very emotional conversation. The reality of it was that I had left her on the hook to tell our family and friends what I had done and to deal with them as well. There were so many things I hadn't thought about before making my move, but things always sound good in theory, and then when you put them into action, they don't always seem to be such bright ideas. I decided to stop for gas and get something to eat. Ahead I found a little gas station with a diner, probably a favorite of truckers along that particular route. The gravel parking lot had seen a lot of action over the years, and as I pulled in the dust came up all around the SUV just like the movies.

I walked into the diner not realizing how hungry I was until I smelled the stale grease and strong coffee. Even in my childhood I'd had a special affinity for greasy-spoon diners, and this was definitely one right out of my dreams. I thought about all the people that had been in and out of here over the years, each bringing a different story as to why they came through. I was just another one of them with my own story, and just like them I would take my story with me.

There were very few customers around, and they paid no attention to me. Most likely they were in deep thought about their lives. Like them I was deep in thought, still trying to understand what had happened and what was going to happen. Sitting on a worn-out stool, with my face down in the palms of my hands, I tried to calm my racing mind.

"Where ya headed?" came a voice from behind the counter. The man addressing me spoke, but it was like I could barely understand the words he was speaking. But strangely enough, I understood what he was saying. He had a strange, almost peculiar-sounding voice, one like I had never heard before. He was an older man with a long beard of yellow and white, stained around the mouth. His hair was long and curly and flowed over his shoulders. As he peered down on me, I felt like he was looking right through me with all of his years of wisdom. There was something in his magical eyes communicating to me, almost as if he already knew me, knew all about me. A shiver ran up my spine. Hesitantly, I looked up and waited a second before responding to his question.

"Oh, just taking a little trip," I said as I picked up the menu to keep from looking in his eyes.

"Trip where?" he asked, probing for an answer.

"I'm headed up to Colorado for a while."

"Well, it should be beautiful this time of year, nice and cool."

"Yes, that's what I hear. Let's see, I think I'll have a cheeseburger basket and a Coke." I hoped my order would discourage further conversation. I wasn't in the mood. I was tired, hungry, and still very confused. I just wanted to eat and wrap my mind around all that was happening. My whole system was still in shock from the news I'd heard just a few days ago.

"Coming right up," he said as he shuffled through the single swinging door to the kitchen. Wondering about who he was or what he was, I couldn't keep from thinking how he just didn't fit in the setting. This whole thing seemed odd. Before I finished my thoughts, his head appeared at the window above the counter where plates of completed orders would be placed if there was a waitress on duty. Mayo or mustard on the burger?

He allowed me to eat my dinner without interruption, and I have to admit it was probably the best burger and fries I'd ever eaten. Even the Coke was cold and refreshing. Or maybe it was just because I had forgotten to eat at all throughout that day. Whatever it was, I felt relaxed yet soothed by the food. It was probably the first time I understood the meaning of the words *comfort food* that Lisa talked about so much. With each bite I felt grateful and took my time enjoying each one.

When I had completed the meal and agreed to a piece of home-made apple pie to go, I asked the old man if I could pay for my gas and food at the same time. He said that would be fine, so I went back outside and filled my gas tank.

"Could you also throw in some of those batteries, please?" I said when I was back inside ready to pay for my purchases.

"Sure, not a problem. I'm sure they'll come in handy if you plan on doing any camping. So you ever been to Colorado before?"

"Nope, it will be my first time." I lied and wasn't even sure why I did.

"A lot of families take vacations up there; see a lot of them come through," he continued as he rang up my purchases. "You meeting your family up there? I noticed your wedding ring."

"Uh, well not this time, just me," I said with some hesitation. It hadn't occurred to me before now that not only was I running away from everyone I knew and loved, but I was doing it alone.

"Well, I'm sure you'll come back a different man. I've heard strange and unusual things sometimes happen up in those moun-tains." His deep blue eyes looked directly into mine and into my soul as he handed me my change. "I look forward to seeing ya again." His smile lit up the room.

I muttered something about being sure I would and turned to walk out the door. Before I could reach it, though, the man spoke again, stopping me in my tracks.

"Take care of yourself, son. I hope you find what you're looking for."

His words haunted me as I got back into the Explorer. The thought of returning, coming back through this way again had not occurred to me. It certainly wasn't in my plan, considering I had terminal cancer. *I'm sure you'll come back a different man ... I've heard strange things happen ... I hope you find what you're looking for ...* Over and over the words he'd spoken played in my head like a record stuck in the jukebox. *Strange things happen ... find what you're looking for ... a different man ... a different man.*

Driving another eighty or ninety miles down the road, I spotted a low-budget motel and realized that the comfort food had also made me comfortably sleepy. I pulled in under the vacancy sign and paid in cash for a room. Nothing fancy was needed on this trip.

The room was clean, although the carpet and bedspread were equally threadbare. As I lay on the soft bed, I realized I hadn't experienced any real pain through the whole day and wondered how bad it would get in the days to come. Just the pains I had days earlier was enough to put me in tears. I couldn't imagine what else was in store for me. All of these things were again possibilities I didn't think about. Before I could ponder that point any further, I was sound asleep. My dreams were filled with all the things I didn't think about before making the decision to leave. Lisa and how she would get through the fact that I had deserted her and the rest of my family. Would I need medication for pain? Would I ever see any of my loved ones again? Would they be able to forgive me? I tossed and turned all night, going in and out of nightmare dreams I was having.

Pulling out of the motel that morning, after a hearty small-town breakfast, I wondered if that would be the last good meal I would ever have. Thinking back at the provisions I had purchased, I was quite sure that it was probably my last real meal.

As I continued to drive, I decided it might be a good time to think about exactly where I was going. All I had thought about was going to the mountains. What mountains? I pulled over and opened the road atlas. South central Colorado appeared to be the least populated, and that's exactly where I wanted to spend my last days, in total seclusion, isolated from everyone and everything that was a part of the life I was leaving behind. I wanted to be one with nature, God, so my eyes, mind, and heart could be opened and my soul could find whatever it was searching for. It felt as if I was being sent on a mission for this reason, genuine soul-searching, on a grand scale.

Late that second night I stopped in another roadside town at the foot of the mountains to eat and sleep. This time I placed the call to Lisa that I had been putting off. The discussion with Lisa was nothing short of gut-wrenching. Without a doubt, it was the hardest thing I had ever done. What words do you use to tell the one you love that you are dying and you're going far away, alone, to die? She cried, and I cried. I could just see her down on her knees in agony. She did her best to convince me to come home, to come back to her and let her take care of me. She begged and pleaded, but I think in the end she knew what I was doing and why I was doing it. We spent some time talking about our lives together and life in general. We talked about Doug and what had happened to him and what I had said at that time. We talked in detail and with passion about the love we had for one another. It was the longest we had talked in years. In the end she hesitantly told me she understood and that she would pray for me; she said, "Go become the eagle I have always seen you as. Go fly and be free." She told me to have courage in facing the demons that would surely be there to battle my intentions. I told her how very much I loved her and thanked her for understanding what I had to do. I just wanted to reach through that phone and hold her, to make right all that I had failed at as a husband. As I hung up the phone, I felt a great peace even though it had been a rough two hours. I felt a detachment from what had been and a new sense of what will be.

Lisa was a strong woman, and she knew where my soul was, but I think she probably thought and hoped that I would come back after a few weeks. I knew in the days to come I would miss her terribly, I would yearn for her, I would beg for her. I would call out her name and doubt myself and my decisions.

As I got closer to Colorado, the landscape quickly started to change. Looking up at the mountains, the fear started to set in. *How am I going to do this? What do I do from here? Where do I start? There are so many things I didn't consider. How will I survive? What will I eat? Where will I stay during the process? What will I do about the elements?* With my eyes half shut, I started to pray.

God, I'm very much alone right now. I'm very scared and confused. I feel so unsure and weak. Everything has happened so quickly. I have prayed to You my whole life, but now I pray out of desperation. Please guide me; show me what to do. Comfort my family and friends. Help me to get closer to You. Please give me the strength and courage to do this because I have to believe that it's You that called me here, summoned me.

I pulled off onto a dirt road and got out of the truck and took in the vast area. The flat prairies were starting to turn into mountains; the oak and elm trees were replaced by cedars and pines. Everything looked different, smelled different, and felt different. There was no noise and no pollution. It was so peaceful, and my soul drank in the purity like a thirsty sponge. I thought back to Doug's last days and wondered if this was what he would have wanted. *Well, Doug, here we are, you and me, doing what we should have done before you left us.* Hopefully you can be here with me at least in spirit.

Then I had a thought, or a thought had me. For each of us living this life, how many more sunrises or sunsets will we see? How many more chances will you have to say I love you and to tell someone how extraordinary and important they are? Why would you not make the decision to start living an extraordinary life right now? What else is more important? Easier said than done!

As I lay on the hood of the car staring up at the Rocky Mountains, I tried to think about the days to come. What would happen to me? What would I become? Would I find the answers I had desperately looked for all my life? What would the last minute of my life be like? I knew that all of these questions, particularly the last one, would be answered in the days to come, but I wasn't afraid.

As I lay there on the hood of my car with the sun in my face, I questioned myself. *What do I want?* How seldom have I ever allowed myself to ask that question, but yet I know you will never have what you don't know you want.

Week One:

THE JOURNEY AND PREPARATION

When I pulled into Telluride I couldn't help but notice all the seemingly happy people on vacation. They were all busy shopping, eating, and trying to relax and forget all the problems at home. On one corner, there stood a group of young people dressed like they were on the verge of extinction, trying to appear oblivious to it all. But I know the dreadlocks and the carefree attitude told a different story. Once when Lisa and I were spending a casual day lounging in downtown Santa Fe, I took the time to talk to a young kid who was a poster child for the young and destitute. After a cup of coffee and a taco, he explained that his father was the CEO of a Fortune Five Hundred company and that his father had chosen a trust fund for him instead of love and being a dad. So the boy became disillusioned with the ideology of big cars, big houses, and eighty-hour work weeks with no parents. None of it made sense to him any longer.

When he had finally decided to leave the comforts of luxury and the drama, his parents didn't even realize he was gone for two weeks. So here he was a millionaire at age nineteen, and he'd never put in one day's work. He didn't know how to take care of himself and had already been in rehab twice. He went on to explain that there were many more like him, all trying to figure out and understand what their purpose in life was. What the meaning of his life was and how to live a life with meaning.

Many kids today look at what we have made out of our lives and try to do something different. The problem is, they just don't know what to do different. No one ever talked to them about how to make their lives successful emotionally, how to be happy and fulfilled. Just look at their role models and what they are, what we are. They're kind of stuck between doing it the way they've seen it done and longing for something different. Then we as a society label them as weird and make things even worse for them.

As I thought about that day, I remembered thinking how lucky I was to have a caring family, a challenging career, and a life that was the envy of many of my friends. Now look at me: alone, confused, and facing death. I wish I could talk to that young man one more time. Though I'm far from having it all figured out, surely there is some way I could help him. Second chances don't often come to a dying man, though, and second chances are opportunity's second knock.

Driving around, I found a parking lot and turned left into it. I found a spot as far back as I could. It didn't take long before the parking lot attendant approached me with a ticket in his hand.

"How long you going to be?" he he inquired. Once again, one of those things I never thought of. I dug through my wallet and pulled out two hundred dollars. At that moment, I wasn't really sure what would happen to my car, but by the time they notified Lisa, it wouldn't matter to me anymore. This would be the best place for it for now.

"Will this buy me some time?" I asked.

"Are you trying to buy time or park your car? If you're trying to buy time, you don't have enough money. Time is on loan to you, son, and all too soon your note will be called in. So use every moment as if it was your last before it's too late."

He took the money and said with a smile, "I'll take good care of her; pick 'er up when you're ready, son, and good luck up there." The sparkle in his eyes mystified me.

I nodded my head, threw my backpack over my shoulder, and started walking. The feeling was nothing short of gut-wrenching despair. I was walking away from the last vestige of my old life, my car. I was getting closer and closer to having no attachments to the life I once knew.

As I continued walking down the road, it all of a sudden dawned on me. That old man looked just like the old man from the gas station yesterday. It couldn't be him, but I could swear it was; surely not. What did he say about being careful up there? I didn't tell him where I was going, and what was that buying time stuff?

I reached the highway after a walk of about a mile and stuck out my thumb. I had never hitchhiked before, and it felt kind of foolish, embarrassing. When I used to see hitchhikers in the past, I'd always thought of them as losers. Now I look and think back and wonder how many of them may have issues much like my own. Maybe they were not losers; maybe they were trying to find their lives as well. You just never know what someone is going through or what their circumstances are.

It didn't take long before a gray-primed truck with big tires and a chrome roll bar pulled over. Inside was a typical young, enthusiastic, adventurous kid, looking like he didn't have a care in the world. His long hair was pulled back in a ponytail. Scattered about in the truck were fishing gear and various pieces of outdoor equipment.

"Need a lift?"

"If you don't mind," I said with somewhat of a hesitant tone.

"Sure, man, climb in." As he stuck out his hand in a gesture to introduce himself, I couldn't help noticing what great energy he had. I wondered what his life was like. Did he have money? Did he have family? Was he happy?

"My name is Noah; what's yours?" he asked with excited enthusiasm.

"Allen. It's nice to meet you, Noah. Where you headed?"

"I'm headed to Denver. Is there anywhere I can drop you?"

There was that question again. *Where* am *I going? If I only knew,* I thought.

"I'm just kind of headed up to the mountains. I'm not really sure exactly where."

"You're in the right place." He smiled. "There're plenty of mountains up here. Are you going camping?"

"Yeah, something like that."

"Be careful," he cautioned. "Although they're beautiful, they can be just as ugly and deadly when they want to, but I'm sure you know what you're doing."

As his truck climbed the winding road, I think he could tell I really didn't want to make new friends. There was, I'm sure, a look on my face that would be hard to understand. After we drove for a while, I started breathing again. This was the first time in a few days that I noticed my lungs working.

Looking out the window, I asked him, "If a person wanted to spend some time by himself for a while, where would be the best place to go?"

"Just up the road a couple of hours there's a valley that leads into a national forest, and it gets pretty remote and gnarly. Not too many people venture up there."

That sounded exactly like what I wanted and needed.

"If you want, I can drop you off there; sounds like what you're looking for. Hey, I never asked you, where you from? You sound like a Texan."

"That obvious, huh? Must be the drawl. I'm from Dallas," I replied. I wanted to ask him some questions about how to survive out there. By the looks of it, he probably had some experience. But I didn't want him to think that I was just another city slicker who was looking to find himself.

As we continued up the winding road, my mind wandered like I was in a dream. *Can I make it? How bad will it get? How long will it take?* I mean, come on, I was really just a city slicker with a bunch of camping gear. It's hard enough for a seasoned outdoors man with years of experience to survive in the mountains. At that moment, I just felt plain silly.

I must have dozed off because I felt a gentle nudge, and my young guide was asking me to wake up. As I opened my eyes, I saw a beautiful valley leading up to the biggest mountain peaks I had ever seen. The trees were dense, and it looked like the beginning of time.

"We're here," Noah said as he pulled over. "This is it. Sure you still want to do this?"

As I opened the truck door, I didn't know whether to thank him or cry.

"Yeah," I said. "I think I do. Thanks for the lift. I appreciate it." Stepping out, I looked up at the vastness of it all. I felt small and insignificant. I felt intimidated.

"Hey, just be careful. Like I said, they may look beautiful, but it's pretty wild up there. Just about anything that can kill you will kill you." I could hear genuine concern in his voice and knew he was probably right.

There was a slight pause as I stood staring, totally awed by the place that I was to call home. I pulled my gear out of the back of his truck and took the first steps into what was sure to be the biggest challenge of my life. "Do you want me to tell someone where you are or something?" he asked, a concerned tinge to his voice.

"No, that's okay. I, uh, really don't need anything; thanks, though," I said, trying to sound more sure and confident of myself than I was feeling.

With a big smile and a wink, Noah pulled away. I don't think I had ever felt the way I did at that moment—scared, excited, and something else I couldn't even describe all at the same time, and what was up with the big smile and wink from Noah? That was strange!

As I began the walk up the valley, I couldn't help noticing the sheer beauty of it all, but I knew soon all this beauty could turn into hell. The question was, would it kill me before the cancer did? Was that what I was hoping would happen? The elements or some wild animal would do for me what I had not been able to do for my friend…pull the plug? Or would I have the chance to do what I needed to do? *And what exactly will I do, or can do,* I wondered. I had no answers to that question or anything else at this point.

The hike in quickly reminded me what the thinner air at such high altitudes can do to your lungs. No matter how physically fit you may think you are, the altitude makes you feel like you are in the worst shape of your life. I slowed my pace to compensate for the thin air and still found myself needing to breathe deeply in an attempt to pull more oxygen into my lungs.

I lost track of time, and before I knew it, it was almost dark. I had been hiking for hours. I started looking around for a place to camp. This would be the place that I would spend my first night. I nestled in between some big rocks that gave some protection and security and unpacked some peanut butter crackers I had bought back in that old gas station that now seemed a million miles away. Now that I thought about it, I realized I hadn't eaten anything all day.

As the chill night air and the dampness from my sweaty clothes started to set in, it dawned on me how quiet it was. The sounds of my own thoughts were like a rock concert, and I had a hard time quieting them down. As the night deepened, my body shivered uncontrollably, and my mind started racing and reeling. What began as a quiet, beautiful mountain evening became a horrifying, cold, noise-filled nightmare. I'm sure it was a combination of fear of what I was doing and fear of where I was. I sat there in a huddled position hour by hour and shook the whole night in a pitiful state. If that was what my first night was like, I dreaded to think what the rest would bring.

Friday

Upon awakening, after what felt like ten minutes of sleep, the world seemed right again. All those horrifying and scary things that had tormented me throughout the night now took their proper places. Kind of like life—one day it seems that everything is out to get you, but with a new day, many of those things just take on another feeling or disappear altogether. That had been my saving grace many times. I'd tell myself to "just get through this day, Allen; tomorrow will look different."

I was amazed to see the things that just hours ago had looked like monsters coming to life as the beauty of the morning unfolded. *My God, this place is beautiful.* The words were resounding in my head and then coming right out of my mouth. As I sat there looking around in amazement, I realized that the only conversations I would be having for a while would be with myself and with my Creator. This, I would have to remind myself, is not crazy.

After pulling what belongings I had together, I made my way down a deep canyon that led to a large meadow at the bottom, stopping only to wash my face and fill up my canteen. I stumbled down the side of the canyon like only a city boy would, making enough noise for the whole world to know I was there.

As I reached the bottom of the canyon, I saw in the distance where the two mountains came together, and in the middle was a very long, deep crevice that was protected from almost every direction. This, I decided, would be the place where I would make my new home.

Although I knew from experience that the distance was much farther than it looked, I was surprised at how different the perspective was from this angle. From where I was standing to where I started this morning was a five-hour hike at a pretty good pace. It just reminded me how small I was in comparison to everything around me. The ascent was even slower; the sides of the canyon were steep and treacherous. Since the pace was slower and I had to stop more often, I had plenty of time to get to know each and every bush in detail. When I had time, I would have to start reading about different food sources that would ultimately sustain me and maybe even help me live longer. The books I bought from the camping store would come in handy up here.

Stumbling and tripping along, I rounded a corner that seemed to welcome me. The view was indescribable. I was centered in the valley, and an incredible sky engulfed the huge mountains that surrounded me. I looked up behind me and saw what looked like a small horseshoe cut into the side of the massive canyon wall. Two very large boulders had fallen away and sat in the middle, which allowed two entrances, one on either side. At the top was an overhang that covered just about three-quarters from the back to the front with a huge tree sitting on top protecting the rest of the open area. It was perfect, and I felt some comfort in that. I had found my new home, my protection, and eventually the place where I would take my last breath. With a few hours of daylight left, I got busy cleaning out and studying my new abode. The next day I would build some gates at both openings to provide a little more security.

The night chill caused me to shiver in my wet, sweaty clothes. I had always dreamed of building a fire pit, and so I did just that. It didn't take long till the warmth and glow of the fire filled the walls of Lazarus Ledge. That's what I decided to call this place, Lazarus Ledge. The Cartwrights had the Ponderosa, the Ewings had South Fork, the Barkleys had Big Valley ranch, and now I had my own, Lazarus Ledge, which was far more special than all the others combined. If I remember the story correctly, Jesus raised Lazarus from the dead. Maybe it's just wishful thinking on my part, but naming this place after a story that offers hope gave me some comfort.

Staring into the fire, a flurry of thoughts filled my mind. Even with the warmth of the now-glowing fire, a strange chill grasped me and took over my weak and tired body. As I began rocking back and forth, my body now shaking uncontrollably, a lone tear ran down my cheek. One by one the tears came until I found myself crying; crying turned to bawling, and the bawling turned into what would be the most intense hours of all my life. As the movie that has been my life played in my mind, every fear I had ever had came pouring out. One by one they overtook me—the fear of living, the fear of dying, fears from childhood, fears of failure, fears of God, and the fear of the uncertainty of what I was doing here in this place so far from my home. Uncontrollably I wept; fears that had accumulated my entire life were rocking the very foundation of my life. These tears were coming from the depths of my soul. I continued to weep uncontrollably, scared of the night, scared of life, scared of the truth, and horrified of the cancer that would end my life.

Saturday

When I awoke this morning after only a few hours of sleep, things seemed a little different. My surroundings looked different. I felt a little better and had a little sense of calm. I had never cried like that in my entire life, and it was very healing. My breathing was deeper, and my mind was clearer. And a lot of the tension in my shoulders was gone. How long had I lived with all these fears? We store in our minds so many things over time that, given the chance to come out, they will. But generally we just keep pushing them deeper and deeper, and eventually they reside in our unconscious mind only, wreaking havoc on our psyche, our bodies, and eventually our lives. Last night was a start, but I'm sure there is much more to come.

Slowly looking around, I started to take in where I was and what I had done. This was when it hit me. Here I was, hundreds of miles from nowhere, like a speck of dust in the Rocky Mountains, dying of cancer. I put my hands over my face, and just as I began to start crying again, I heard a voice in my head, a very faint voice. It said, *Allen, you are a spiritual being living a human experience. This is your chance to find your soul, your spirit. Leave the man/human reality behind; become aware of the thing that has been beckoning you your whole life. It is at hand.*

Though I didn't totally understand this statement, I felt like it was something I needed to remember and that I would understand its meaning in the days to come.

I began to realize how real all this was, not just one of those many things I had thought about starting or doing many times. My head came up. Something was different, an unfamiliar confidence, a purpose, like I had never felt before. Somehow I felt like I could do it, I could make it. This was my one chance in life. Something I had to see to the end, literally.

The morning was cool and crisp. I stoked what was left of the fire that had sent me into oblivion earlier that night and let the heat warm my chilled bones. I couldn't keep from smiling as I thought about how I felt at that exact moment, as new sense of purpose filled my mind, the kind I had searched for all of my life. All the fears that I had experienced just hours ago were now somehow left in the embers at my feet. Now I wondered what else was in store for me. What I wanted was the truth about my life, the truth about God, the truth about living. I just want the truth!

After eating a prepackaged breakfast, it was time to start building my new home. Carefully, I studied the landscape and the place I had selected and named. Already I felt at home on Lazarus Ledge, like I'd been there before or it had been waiting for me, hidden away in my psyche somewhere. It was more than just a shelter. It had been created for me. I was sure. It had been waiting for me all these years, waiting for me to fulfill my purpose. Yes, I suddenly knew I, Allen, had a purpose. I still wasn't sure what the purpose was, but sitting in my new shelter, I was sure for the first time that this life was filled with purpose and meaning. I now understood that the only meaning in life was the meaning of the very moment you were in. How you choose to experience it, how you choose to feel it. The meaning to life was not something that you would somehow find around a corner. It was not something that would just magically appear. The only meaning was the meaning you gave to it at any given moment.

As I thought more about purpose and meaning of life, one thing that I could not get out of my mind was the process of living life and chasing happiness, chasing purpose. Happiness is so fleeting, so temporary. It never lasts. If you get that new car you thought would make you happy, the feeling is gone in days. The raise at work or the vacation you have been waiting on as well. Everything that you think will make you happy somehow just adds to the problem. Because once the happiness feeling is gone, you are left with even more yearning, more confusion on what it will be that will sustain that feeling of contentment. There has to be more to life than our life hinging on a word like *happiness.*

What I wanted was to find my highest self, the thing that would transcend happiness. What I sought after would be lasting and permanent. Something I didn't have to think about but just simply was. This was what it would look like, sound like, and feel like. I would be transparent. I would be rested. I would be at peace, focused, forgiving, loving, patient, wise, sure, creative, powerful, inspired, energetic, and empowered. It would no longer just be a feeling I was chasing but more like living in a sense of joy and appreciation of being alive.

My home had everything I would need: protection from the environment, protection from the animals, and a place to plan my metamorphosis and eventually the last moment of my life. I rolled up my sleeves and dove right in to the new project of fixing up my home. After an hour or so, most of the limbs and mountain trash were cleared out and the floor brushed clean. On either side of the boulder that sat in the middle of the horseshoe entrance was a small opening that would need to be sealed up if there was to be total protection from the outside. At the opening on the left, I piled up rocks and large tree limbs to close it in so there would only be one way in and out. Though I felt more acclimated to the altitude than the day before, my lungs burned like my first cigarette when I was just eleven. But each rock I laid on top of the other seemed to give my arms more strength and purpose.

As the sweat dripped from my forehead, I had to think this was the first real physical labor that this body had seen since my firewood delivery days in college. By now, the sun glared from high above with great intensity, and my screaming muscles called for a break. In all the focus to get here and to build my new home, I had let a lot of the breathtaking beauty of this place escape me. I sat back and admired this incredible place. The mountains that surrounded me were absolutely stunning. The tall peaks reached up and touched the sky, and the deep canyons were rugged and dangerous. The trees that clung to the steep sides were overwhelmingly majestic. The air was cool and crisp, and the only noise was that of life.

I should have moved Lisa out of the city and to a place like this years ago, I thought. But the trappings of a good job, nice house, and new cars were like golden handcuffs. How many times did we plan our escape over a glass of wine? We would build a small home and live a simple life. I would work at a local lumberyard, and Lisa would work at a café. We dreamed a lot, talked a lot, but six years later, settled in and much more in debt, all that we created left us shackled to an existence that we loathed.

As I let the magic of this place soak in, I thought, felt, and heard these words:

From the stars in the heavens to the forest floor, to the tallest of peaks and the deepest of valleys, everything above and everything below is there for your enjoyment, your pleasure, and for you to know I, your God, exist and love you. I call it free will, love, wonder, and contemplation. These four things are what separate you from everything else and are my greatest gifts to you.

Like before, I was not really sure where those words came from, but deep inside I had a hope, a want, and a desire. All I could think to say at the moment was again, "Thank you!"

As I sat back and loved the beauty of what I was seeing all around me and wondering, contemplating it all, I noticed something. I was aware of something more than my brain working. I was aware of my thoughts separate from my mind, something outside of my body. In fact, I noticed that each time I did those things my eyes fixed on something and my brain stopped thinking for that moment and something else happened. I was conscious of me, the thing that is not my body and not my mind. It was the real me. I laid back and reveled in the moment, never wanting to forget it.

After a while I continued my work, and my thoughts turned to home. What is my family doing now? Are they worried sick? Are they out looking for me? Are they scared? I can only imagine the torment they must be going through, wondering how I could have left them. What are the people at work saying and thinking? Just like them, this will be one of the hardest things I will have to come to grips with. For now, I will have to trust myself and God and know this is the right thing for me to do.

As the work began on the second opening, which included a door made from branches and thick bark that would be my door to the entrance, I noticed some curious onlookers, probably wondering what this crazy man was doing. Not sure what kind of animals they were, but they looked like large gophers, each chirping as if to tell me I was doing it wrong. I hope I don't end up having to eat one someday.

I must say that I had always been pretty creative and resourceful when I needed to be in my life. The door worked perfectly, and as I stood back to admire the fine work, once again an uncommon strength and profound sense of purpose filled my mind and body. I will need that strength and more in days to come, I'm sure.

ON THE LEDGE OF LIFE

Walking back inside my new home, I felt good about what I had created. There was a strong sense of accomplishment and peace with my dwelling. Not like the safety of a brick house, more like the safety of a mother's arms.

It was time to unpack and organize the few belongings that I brought on the journey. I waited for the fire to reach the perfect blaze. It was a very strange feeling as I started pulling things out of my bags. I didn't even remember what I'd bought at the sporting goods store. I had just grabbed whatever looked like what I might need. *In the end,* I had thought, *it really won't matter anyway.* I would just as soon leave nothing behind but my footprints in the sand.

As I spread everything out on the ground, I realized how good this simple life really felt. We truly do live with so much clutter in our lives. We continue to accumulate but rarely let go of anything. We just have so much stuff and seldom use any of it. All these possessions just add to the clutter in our minds. Each item meant survival to me. Matches meant fire and warmth. The fishing kit meant food. The knife meant protection. The wilderness survival book was knowledge, and the Bible that I took from the motel meant truth. Some of the other items, like the camping cook pots, were just simple luxuries.

This all reminded me of when I was determined to join the Boy Scouts as a kid. I dragged my mother down to Gibson's and bought everything on the list provided by the Scout Master. My poor mother, being single and without much money, did all she could for me. She probably felt sorry for me since I had no father in my life. Three days after joining I quit, and she never said a word. I wish she would have made me stick it out. This, like so many other things in my life, I was allowed to start and then quit. As much as I love my mother and all she tried to do for me, I wish she would have been a little harder on me and not been so worried that I wouldn't like her if she chose to be a little tough on me. I've finally come to the one thing I cannot quit.

I started thinking about all the things I had quit in my life and why. Why do we start so many things only to quit them shortly after? There was a long list for me. Diets, exercise programs, multi-level business adventures, karate lessons, guitar lessons, abstaining from drinking, the list goes on and on. I could blame a lot of things, but at some point I needed to start taking responsibility for my own failure to follow through. The lack of self-discipline we all have in our lives keeps us looking back wondering. Now looking back at the Boys Scout failure, which would have really helped me, I saw the reason was just a lack of commitment, no accountability to me and the others in my life. If Lisa and I would have had children, I believe I would have been more encouraging to them to see things through to the end. I would have made them commit to things and not quit. The only thing that I had not quit up to this point was my marriage, but maybe I had done that as well. Now I just looked back and felt shame. If only I had . . .

I'd always been an organizational freak who had to have everything in its place, probably to overcompensate for the rest of my life being a mess. Maybe it was because I felt that those were things I could control, and if I immersed myself in those small tasks, I wouldn't have to think about anything else.

When everything started coming together, Lazarus's Ledge almost felt homely. As I sat and examined all of what I had done, there was one thing missing: a calendar. Everyone knows you have to keep track of time. For me, time was more like a goal, not a cumulative sequence of history. On the side of the wall, I went to work smoothing an area where an X would be an accounting of the days and nights of this process. When the X marks ended, I would be gone.

That night as I stared into the fire, the question of life and what we have made of this life started to come clear. Look at how we have created this illusion that if you spend your life in the pursuit of money and success you will be happy. I thought back, and if you look at the time it takes to finish college and then work your way up in a company to the point where you are actually making more than it takes to survive, half your life is over, and you're still in debt and have less time than ever. Your kids are grown, you've lost the best years of your physical life, and now everything you have accomplished means very little.

Life just kind of passes us by. Somehow our priorities just get screwed up. We forget what is important, like spending time being in love with life, admiring the beauty all around us, our health, our families, our dreams. How about actually teaching your kids about life instead of making that the job of schoolteachers? We make sure they can do algebra and chemistry. We make them pass tests and fulfill all the curriculum before they can graduate, as if all or any of that will help them live a wonderful life. But we spend very little time, if any, on how to live a happy, well-adjusted life. We don't teach them, and just like everything else, they have to learn and understand how to live a great life. If we are not going to do it, then we should have life teachers in the schools that explore and teach about how to live a great life…a life mentor. Why would that not be just as important? I don't remember anything about geometry, but I would have remembered if someone had skilled me on how to be happy. How many struggles could I have avoided if someone would have showed me how?

Look at what all of this has come to. The goal is to live the American dream, drive an expensive car, live in a big house with a pool, wear designer clothes, and own a vacation home. We do things to our bodies that kill us, and everyone pretends it's not happening; we just won't acknowledge it. We use love like it's a drive-thru, fast-food restaurant, whatever tastes good that day, and at the end of the day, enough is never enough. No wonder our kids grow up confused and misguided, and we put them on medication and hope for the best, thinking it's a chemical defect in their bodies. In the pursuit of all that we think will bring us happiness, we subject ourselves to stress, anxiety, and overindulgence; then, like our kids, we take pills to help us forget, forgive, and feel good. We take a pill to sleep, we take a pill to stay awake, and we take a pill to change how we feel during the time in between. Does any of this make sense?

Why is it that we all know better but continue down the same track? Are we just hoping someone, something, will come along and stop the misery? When Doug died, I remember him saying to me in one of his conscious moments, "Allen, don't be sad for me. I did this to myself. Even though I knew the things I was doing to my body would kill me someday, I did them anyway. I let life just pass me by. I never addressed the things that caused me so much confusion and drama. Don't let it happen to you; make changes in your life, and if it does happen to you, don't end up like me dying and not even aware of it most of the time."

I remember so many nights sitting by his bed wishing I had the courage to end it for him. I remember the night he held my hand and begged me to unplug the machines and let him go. He would say, "Allen, this is no way for a man to die. It's not natural. I feel like I should have died in some kind of battle or fight. Like a warrior with no shame, no regrets." The look on his face said it all.

I know that what I'm doing will be looked at in many different ways. Some will call me a coward, some will say how selfish I was, and most will just say I was crazy, but I want to know that exact moment when I leave this world and meet my Creator in heaven. I want to be aware of the last thing I see before I draw my last breath. I want to smile as I think about the life I lived, and I want to say thank you to life.

I started praying, *God, forgive my soul for all that I have done and not done. I ask forgiveness from all the people I have hurt. Cleanse my mind, purify my body, and take from my mind all the voices. Let these last days of my life be in peace and calm; may the pain that will come give me life. My God, I am here. Be with me and open my eyes to all that I have missed and not understood. Let these days prepare me for my death so that when I see my last moment I will die fully alive. Amen.*

Change has got to be one of the hardest things to do. For most of us, we spend our whole lives trying to implement changes with very little success. It has always been very confusing to me why we just can't make the changes we desire and make the changes last. We try to quit smoking, eat healthier, get on an exercise program, get up earlier, watch less TV, but just can't seem to make the changes last. It all seems so easy. I think that we just have so many other things competing for our attention that we can't focus on any one thing long enough, so the easy thing to do is to fall back on the habits we are trying to change; then we have one less thing to focus on and think about. The changes we can and should make in our lives could lead to such greatness. But we choose instead immediate gratification, and we don't worry about the eventual outcome.

The changes that I was getting ready to make were going to be on a galactic scale. There was no more nicotine, TV, liquor, or unhealthy food available. I would have to focus like I never had. I would have to change! I had no choice! Maybe I should have chosen differently when I had a choice. Now *there's* a thought. We have a choice. It's just too bad it had to get to this before I realized it. I too had been given choices.

How do we make these changes in our lives? How do we become something we are not or we think we're not? Through the years, each time I tried to change something and failed, I became weaker, and that made it harder the next time I tried to change something. I would stop believing I had any power over my life, any choice. I read lots of self-help books over the years, but when I look back, I realize they made very little difference in my life, not because they didn't have the answers, but because I refused to do anything with the knowledge that was in them.

Here is the truth. Most of us complain about everything. Rarely are we part of the solution, just the problem. We lack commitment, and we are not very deliberate about our lives. We walk around with crossed fingers, hoping everything will work out. I think a lot of it comes from the attention we get by having more issues than the next guy. It's like we want people to know the burdens we carry, even if we created them ourselves. The truth just becomes part of the lies.

Great things come from changes. Great things come from the actions of changes. The problem is that we have a very difficult time committing to those things that would change our lives. Without the commitment, we live with hesitation, so we have one foot in and one foot out of life. Most of my friends and I expected great things from our lives but were unwilling to pull the switch to make the changes necessary to achieve success.

I laid back and started listing in my mind all the things I would have changed. They started mounting up. I would have changed:

I would have slept and rested more.

I would have turned my TV off.

I would have meditated more.

I would have gotten up earlier.

I would have read more.

I would have taken piano lessons.

I would have saved more money.

I would have eaten better and exercised more.

I would have spent more time with my family and friends.

I would have finished the Boy Scouts.

I would have been more committed to the success of my life.

I would have learned more about the stars and constellations.

I would have spent more time helping others.

I would have spent more time outdoors.

I would have communicated better.

I would have let go of my ego and pride.

I would have loved more.

I would have had higher expectations of myself and my life.

So here it was, the most tragic statement of all. If I would have, if I had only, why didn't I? Right now I just wish that I had the chance to do it over again. I would make these changes, no matter what. How different would my life have been?

Why is it that even though we are the authors of our own lives, we continue to write scripts that don't reflect what we really want? As the authors of our lives we can and should make the decisions on how we want our lives to look, feel, and ultimately be. Why don't we write the stories to be exactly how we want them? We somehow let others write the scripts for us, or we don't take care how we edit and rewrite how we would want our lives to read. How crazy is that? How could we let that happen? Tomorrow when you get wake up, you get to write the script of how you will feel, how you will look at things, and how you will experience your day. You might not get to write what will happen, when and where, but you can decide how you will react to what does.

I decided to write a one-page script on what my life was and what I wanted it to be:

> Allen was and is a good man. He tried for most of his life to be happy and have a successful life. But, like a lot of people, he knew life just seemed to always be a constant struggle and battle. Day after day he tried to make good decisions and get his life together. There were times he tried to eat healthy and to take care of his body. There were times he tried to work on his life path, and there were times he knew what his priorities were and what was important.
>
> Month after month for the many years, he just always felt an unrest, an uneasiness that kept him wondering and waiting for something to happen that would make all the necessary changes that he so desperately wanted and needed that would last. He kept waiting and seeking, and though there were moments that it seemed that all was great in his life, they were generally temporary, and he would find himself right back were he started.

Allen had many friends and was well liked by others, but relationships always were very hard for him. He seemed to always be let down or let down those he loved. From the outside, people would think he had it great, that he had it all together, but for Allen, there could have not been anything further from the truth.

Peace, contentment, love, success, truth, and happiness were the things that he desired. He read all the books that promised answers. He went to church on occasion and talked to people that he trusted, looking for the answer. Still he found himself waiting, longing.

Allen would think that it just couldn't be that hard. That the answers he sought were just around the corner, in the next book, or the next battle won. And he also feared that this was just how life was going to be, that there was nothing better than what he had, and he would just have to accept that. He left life up to chance, not understanding that he had a say in it.

So much time wasted on such unnecessary thoughts and self-sabotage. There was so much unnecessary pain and hurt. Looking back, Allen realized that it all could have been different! His emotions did not have to dictate his actions.

Now with so many what ifs and if I had onlys, there were some decisions to make to save the life that was left. It took a tragic event in his life for him to define and recreate what Allen, the author of his life, would choose to bring to paper. Just that realization and opportunity in those thoughts are life changing in themselves. To take responsibility for the chapters to come and what they would look like.

Maybe the answers will come to me later when I'm forced to stare them in the face. And maybe, with all that I now realize, there will be a chance to course correct. I will write the future with intent.

Week Two:

EXPLORING AND LEARNING TO SURVIVE

Sunday

Morning came with the sound of life all around me. The sun felt good on my chilled body, and the air was crisp and clean. There were no other humans for hundreds of miles, and I liked the thought of that. As I lay there looking at my newly created home, again a sense of pride filled me. Although I had put in many hard days working, my body felt strong and nimble, and even though I had spent most of the night staring into the fire and contemplating life, I felt rested and powerful. It seemed as though my mind was clearer and my body was stronger for the moment.

I spent some time focusing on living in the moment, the present, the here and now. Most of our lives are spent in living in the past or the future. We all get so busy with yesterday and tomorrow that the present ceases to exist. There is something so powerful in just living and being focused in this moment; it truly does bring so much clarity to things. I remember many times when days would go by and I felt like I had just lost them. Weeks and months became just a blur. How many times did I say and hear others say, "Man, is it November already?" It seems we forget we won't be here forever. From this day forward, I decided I would live every moment. I would truly see things with my eyes, truly feel them as I held them in my hands. I would be aware of me.

Now that I was dying, I wanted to live life in the now, and I saw that living life now is not something that happens to you; it's a decision you make. Instead of waking up in the morning and trying to figure out how we are going to make it through the day, maybe we should determine, make the decision on how we are going to experience the day, the way we want to, moment by moment. Truly create what your day will feel like, look like, and become.

The wounds we carry around from the past and the wounds we create for the future keep us from truly living a life based on the present moment. . How many hours and days have we all wasted contemplating things that have happened or will happen, things we can't change? The fact is that whatever happened is over and done with, and what will happen will be over and done with as well as soon as it happens. Most of the time we don't pay attention to what is happening now because we are so absorbed in yesterday or the days to come. Then we look back and wish we had paid more attention, and we start dealing with what we didn't pay attention to in the first place. This is the vicious circle we create and live in.

So with that in mind I wrote:

When I was young my father's blood-stained eyes scared me.

Was it the whisky, lack of sleep, and worry that did this?

I know his once blue eyes sang with love and excitement.

Now with the days past added up, they drip with the pains of yesterday.

My gaze into the mirror future reveals the start of my own set of cloudy, hazy, sleepless moments, once gleaming with hope and confidence, now giving way to doubt and regret.

Years to come. I will most certainly share the same fate as he.

How many others will create the same honor?

Is there a cure, or is it too late?

Fill my eyes with light, my giving Father, or pluck them from my head.

I don't want to give to others the right to say what a man, how much he must have given, went without.

Now look at him, young, but in his gaze.

How many must have benefited from his soul.

Lost is his power. Lost is his power.

There is a lot that can be achieved in our lives by asking ourselves good, clear, exact questions. The reason that we don't might be because of the answers we will get back. We have the answers to most of life's issues; we have the answers to most of our problems, but because we will have to take responsibility for the answers, we just don't ask. Living with that knowledge of the truth is worse than just not asking. We live our lives preferring not to take ownership of the truth because then it requires us to take action or live with the guilt. Lying to ourselves is even easier than lying to our friends and family. And if you can pretend well enough that you don't have the answers, who can blame you for the issues at hand? Thus, we live our lives convincing ourselves and the people around us that it is something or someone else's fault.

As I thought about that truth, I asked myself the question that has been haunting me day and night. "Why is my marriage not right? What is my part; what is my responsibility?" As soon as I asked that question, I felt a knot in my stomach, and the answer came. *Allen, you quit treating your wife like your wife; you started treating her like your employee. You developed expectations, along with rules and guidelines. You forgot her purpose in your life; you forgot what made her so special to you. You stopped putting your marriage before all things. You left God out of your marriage.* God, the truth hurts, but taking responsibility for your part in life is where it all begins.

With that I started to ask myself some of the questions that I was afraid to ask before.

Why am I so afraid of change?

Why do I live with so much fear?

Why don't I commit my life to God?

Why do I have insecurities?

Why can't I let go of the past?

Why am I afraid to take chances?

Why do I take things people say so personally?

As I shined the flashlight into the depths of my mind, the answers came one by one, and they all had a common thread: fear—fear of failure, fear of being exposed, fear of being found out for what I really am. So as I looked back on my life, I was really living a big lie. Almost everything I did was a cover-up and a mask. Had I ever been my true self? I wish I would have asked these questions a long time ago. It felt good to see and except the responsibility of me and my actions.

Monday

My new home still needed some tender, loving care, but I decided to spend a day exploring and getting used to my new surroundings. I needed to get a good feel for location markers and distances. I knew from past experiences that things are not always what they seem in the mountains. It's easy to get lost, and the distance is always twice what you thought.

I grabbed some jerky and my belt bag, along with my knife, canteen, compass, and a few other odds and ends, and started walking back down toward the stream below. My lungs were still not acclimated to the altitude, and they strained with each step. It would take a few more days before I didn't have to stop every hundred feet and catch my breath. I felt like a tractor mowing my way through the woods, slipping on every rock, getting hung up on every branch. It made me feel like I didn't belong here, as if every animal around me was laughing at me, or worse, hunting me.

The creek was running fast and had a lot of water in it. The sound of the running water helped dilute all the noise I was making and helped me feel more at ease. As I splashed the cold mountain water on my face, I remembered that all the books had said to not drink the water even though it was clear as tap water. They said you should always boil the water or use purification tablets because of the bacteria that can cause some severe problems and even death. In years past, I always drank from the running streams, thinking that before we had running water treated with chemicals people had survived from drinking the water from lakes, rivers, and streams for a long time. Lisa would always get so mad and say, "If you get sick and ruin our trip, I'm not taking care of you," and I would torment her as I was sticking my face down in the water and drinking my fill. I never got sick and for some reason always felt that the fresh, snow-melted water filled with minerals made me stronger and more connected to mother earth.

The sound of the rippling water was calming, and the cool morning breeze across my damp face felt wonderful, refreshing. I sat down and built a fire with my magnifying glass that came with my all-in-one camper's survival knife set and decided to take a little nap and just enjoy the moment. As always, my mind drifted. How many Native Americans had walked by this same creek in the past, drinking, hunting, building the things they would need to survive? How many millions of years did it take to create this place? How many years would it take for humans to destroy this place? Why did we allow this to happen? How could we be okay with what we were doing to the environment? How could we just ignore it? It made me sick at my stomach to know that I had been a part of this destruction. As I thought about that, it reminded me of a show I watched on caves all around the world. Left untouched by humans, the beauty almost defied belief. Unscathed, they remained with no scars created by our ravenous hunger to impact.

More and more my thoughts continued to wander back to everyone back home. *What are my wife and family doing this very moment? Are they going about their business, working, paying bills, mowing the lawn?* God, I really missed them; it was almost unbearable if I thought about them for too long. You truly didn't know what you had until it was gone!

I pulled myself up, put out the fire, and began my hike again. This was going to be fun. I loved exploring, looking in the creeks for trout, finding bones from animals that had met their last day, and marveling at all the strange and unusual things that had been created by millions of years of evolution. Hiking in the mountains was like yoga times ten. You had to stretch, reach, and balance yourself with every step. With every step I could feel the years of sedentary lifestyle being torn away. It took a long time to get very far because nothing was a straight shot. You went up a little ways, back down, then left, and then right just to get a hundred yards. By the time you got from point A to point B, you have added almost half the distance.

I had traveled about a mile or two when the creek turned into a small waterfall. It dropped down about twenty feet or so to a large pool of water. I made a quick mental note to remember this place because it was going to be so much fun to jump into later. Then I remembered that later was not as much of an option any longer. *There is no time like the present. Live in the moment, Allen.* I took my bag off, threw it down, and, with a yelp, jumped. The water was so cold that when I landed it felt like I had landed in a bed of stickers.

When I got to the bank, I just sat there and laughed. How many times in our lives do we miss out on an opportunity to feel alive, to do something that really makes us feel on fire? I was proud that I didn't let this one pass by. For the moment, I felt alive.

It was getting close to noon and the sun was warm and bright; the rays of sun felt good on my cold body. I lay there for the next two hours napping and admiring all the beauty that surrounded me; this place was so beautiful. I wondered how life would have been had I grown up in a place like this. I always thought that I lived in the wrong time. I would have made a great explorer or cowboy or something. Pulling some beef jerky out of my bag, I thought about what it would have been like to have lived like a Native American. What did they think about? What were their problems before the white man came along and destroyed their lifestyle?

Remembering how quickly the sun goes down in the mountains, I started the trek back. I didn't know my surroundings well enough to get caught in the dark. One wrong step could be my last. No need to hasten my end.

Even though it wasn't the Hilton, Lazarus Ledge already felt safe and comfortable, and I was glad when I got back and settled myself in. After cleaning up and building a temporary cot that would keep me off the ground, I fell fast asleep. The fresh air and unhurried exploration had done me a world of good. But that night I had strange dreams, dreams of people I didn't know and places I had never seen before. In each dream, there was a hazy look to everything. In all the dreams, the people never knew I was there, kind of like I was just an observer. In one dream, I could look up at them or down at them and sometimes right through them. I saw these people living their days and how insignificant their lives were. They were just putting one foot in front of the other. Living without purpose and intent, they just survived the days. It looked all too familiar. I watched them perform their daily task, and I thought if they only knew how lucky they were right now. I longed for the tasks that I used to think were so laborious, like going to the store for Lisa, going through the mail, and doing the dishes.

Tuesday

I slept hard and long. When I awoke, it felt like I had slept for more than twelve hours, and when I checked, it had not been that far off. I had slept for eleven hours and fifteen minutes. This was remarkable and noted here because sleep had been foreign to me most of my life. I had, at times, survived without sleep for as much as four days. Most nights I would average three to six hours, and over time the lack of sleep had affected not only my mind but my body as well. Maybe this had contributed to what was now eating my body up inside. The near twelve-hour sleep I experienced was amazingly rejuvenating. I couldn't remember when I felt as strong and alert, and I wondered if this was how most people feel every day. I wish it could have come sooner.

Because this was such a unique experience for me, I ruminated for a while on the concept of sleep and its restorative powers. Sleeping problems seemed to be plaguing all of our society. A lot of my friends had confessed to having problems similar to mine. For me, the problem was that I just couldn't turn my mind off, like it was trying to catch up with all the things that were going on in my life. Like most everyone else, there was just so much for my mind to deal with. Like a lot of other urbanites, I tried taking sleeping pills, but I found that they dulled my senses and made me feel even more tired the next day. The same thing happened with alcohol. Neither of these unnatural methods of going to sleep allowed my mind and body to get what it needed most: natural rest. It just didn't make sense that I would need to take a pill to get to sleep so I could wake up feeling as badly as if I had not slept at all.

In spite of the fact that I was still dying of cancer, the awesome experience of a long, relaxing, life-giving sleep gave me new hope and energy.

In looking around my new homeland, it continued to amaze me how beautiful this place really was. After a quick breakfast of some peanuts and a can of sardines, I took off in the direction of a rock outcropping on the other side of the canyon that I had been admiring since day one.

In this, my second week as a wilderness survivor, my lungs were starting to get acclimated to the altitude, and my pace was starting to quicken. My steps were becoming surer, and my balance was getting much better. I remembered a movie I once saw where a hunter who was living up in the mountains used to talk to himself out loud while walking, probably to keep from going crazy. While I was walking, it dawned on me that I had not spoken a word out loud in days. So I figured, why not? It's not like anyone is going to be listening or pointing at me like I'm some kind of weirdo. That's a societal thing, not a nature-child thing. So I prayed out loud and at the top of my voice as if God couldn't hear me.

"God, be with me today. I believe You brought me here for a reason, so I am going to leave my health and my safety in Your hands. You seem to know what You're doing. Please take care of my family. I know they must be worried and scared. Please help them understand what I have done, and while You're at it, help me understand what I have done. I know You'll bless the lives of those closest to me with happiness, health, peace, and love because they have suffered enough pain through me. Be with me, and open my mind and soul to what I need to hear and experience."

Walking through the woods in the mountains, one will find the myriad signs of the circle of life. Deer and elk bones litter the ground. It had always given me an eerie feeling when I came across a carcass that was fairly fresh. I didn't know if it was the fear of what killed it or just that death was hitting too close to home. But in my present situation, I was starting to see things differently. I saw it as the beauty of the life cycle. In the animal kingdom, there was a natural way that death came, and for some reason I felt, I hoped, that the animal that gave his life felt no pain, no fear. I sat down and thought for a while about the moment that the deer I came across that morning transcended from this life to the next.

Did God take the animals too? Or were they just part of the earth, like the rocks and dirt and water? It was hard for me to imagine that God created all these things but wouldn't want them to come back to Him when their lives were finished. Each animal, each tree, each plant had a purpose, and when that purpose was fulfilled, there must be more. A reward should be given for having lived and died in support of the continuation of life. I had to believe in God as loving everything and everyone; therefore, I would probably be seeing that same deer on the other side of the veil of life and death one day soon. I hoped he remembered me because I wanted to tell him how beautiful he was lying there in the morning sun on a mountain on earth. He and I had become connected in this singular moment, sharing the moment though one of us was dead already and the other was still looking for the door. That's when I had my next revelation.

All things under heaven and created by God were connected. This gave me such a sense of purpose because when you have kinship you have responsibility. Wow! This was an awesome feeling. I was a part of something very, very huge. I was a part of the entire cycle of life that God created, and I had a purpose. He, the God of all creation, knew me, thought about me and that deer and everything else around us, and created us to be a part of each other's lives.

Wednesday

I had always been a reader, mostly spiritual books and self-help books. I believed that if one sentence increased the quality of my life, even for a moment, then it was worth reading. One of my favorite books was *Conversations with God*. It was like God was talking to me in that book, and whether or not it was a true account, the words made sense to me and coincided with the way I thought about God and spirituality. My next favorite was *As a Man Thinketh*. That book was truly my all-time favorite, and I had given it to many people as gifts. I had also recently picked up the Bible and started reading it again. The more I read it, the more I wondered about the life I was living and if I was doing it right. Although I considered myself a Christian, according to the Bible, I was still living a life of sin that would keep me from the pearly gates someday. I pray I get some clarity about this somehow, before I find out the hard way!

It seemed like I had suffered from some kind of instability or lack of peace for most of my life and searched desperately for the answers that would change my life. There were just too many days I felt this unrest and concern. I never really could appreciate any success I had; it was just never enough. The successes I did have were always short lived, and then I would want something else, something different. As I said before, I would read books, meditate, and talk to anyone I thought could shed some light on the matter. Mostly I stayed confused and stayed in a constant state of searching.

For most of my life, I had always had a strong belief in God—not in the traditional, conventional, business style of church belief but a day-to-day knowing that my being here was no accident and that the life in me did not come from evolution. It always seemed to me that there was truth in both evolution and creation. I never believed in the hell, fire, and damnation that so many fundamentalist churches preached or brainwashed people into believing. To me, that was just like advertising, and this was what they wanted you to fear. The truth was, just like everyone else, I didn't know what happened when you died. I just hoped I saw God on the other side. How could anyone ever really know the answers to all this? I prayed the answers would come.

God was beautiful to me, and I didn't know what my life would be like without my belief in Him. More and more though, I had been starting to believe that the Bible was the source and that the words written were the truth even though I had struggled with this concept most of my life. I mean, what was the worst thing that would happen to you if you followed the teachings of Jesus? You would cut out the things that poison your body, treat people better, love more, and have less drama. If, for whatever reason, it was not true, you wouldn't miss anything and your life would still be better for it. Soon enough I would know what the truth really was.

As I hiked, I made sure to get a good feel for where I was, looking for markers and points that I would use to find my way back to my camp. Getting lost in the mountains was extremely dangerous. Many people had died from dehydration and cold just because they didn't pay attention to where they were going, where they had been, and how to return. They got lost. It's quite easy to do because everything starts looking the same, kind of like life if you're not paying attention to the details. Every day we just pass right by or ignore some of the most wonderful things in our lives. Everything looks the same in the mountains. The trick I found was to follow the valleys and look for large markers overhead. It wouldn't take long until I became like the animals native to the area, guiding myself by feel and touch and that third sense that most of us lost thousands of years ago from lack of use.

Food was always a priority, and I knew the supplies I brought would soon run out. I didn't want to die of starvation before the cancer had its chance to take me. But it could boil down to just that, a contest between what got me first—a fall from a cliff, an attack from a wild animal, a snake bite, starvation, or the disease. I wondered why I had not been experiencing digestive problems since the liver was so important to that function. Maybe it was because I was eating very little that was fatty or that would irritate the liver.

Life, diet, and survival were starting to take on a different reality. No more stopping at McDonald's or opening the refrigerator and grabbing a sandwich. No more procrastination, waiting until next week. This was just pure minute-by-minute survival in the purest form. Created by God and created, I feel, just for me.

As a young man, I often dreamt that someday I would have a chance to rough it and to make it on my own. Little did I realize back then that the day would come but for an entirely different reason. I wasn't here to learn to survive. I was here to learn how to die with dignity, peace, and to find the truth of life. I also was here to come to a conclusion on my beliefs on God and religion.

For the first time since seeing the oncologist and hearing the diagnosis, I silently admitted to God, to the universe, and to myself that I wanted to live. At least live while I was alive.

As I continued up and down the canyons and through the creeks, I remembered the book I had bought as a teen on how to survive in the wild. I sure wished I'd read that book; I'm sure that this would have been much easier with a little more knowledge. For now, I just needed to pay attention to the plants and animals living around me and mark places to watch for on my return trip. For the most part I was going to learn on the fly and hope that I didn't make a lethal mistake.

I had probably seen more than fifty deer and rabbits, and squirrels seemed to be everywhere. I knew there were trout in the streams. Thinking of the trout brought back memories of Lisa.

She and I were on a hiking trip to Lake City, and as we walked along a stream, I figured out how to see the trout. You have to fix your eyes in a spot and then see with your peripheral vision. Trout are very nervous fish, and they see everything. They blend in very well in their surroundings, making it hard to be seen. I was standing on a rock with my walking stick that I had whittled a rather nice point on the end of, so when I saw a good-sized trout hiding in the shade in some calm waters, my first instinct was to take a stab at it and cook it up for dinner. That's the macho-male, hunter ego working. Lisa had a fit that I was going to kill such a beautiful creature just so I could say I did it. After a somewhat lengthy debate, I yielded and moved on, thinking I would return alone next time and prove my manliness when she was not around to watch. I never did go back to that stream or try to get that fish. Somehow Lisa's side of the argument made a whole lot more sense after a sunset in the cabin we rented, nestled together on a big feather bed.

Now I was faced with the need to stay alive, and in order to do that, I would have to partake of the gifts God had given me, including that trout. There was no time like the present. Fresh fish for dinner would be a welcome change, and I was going to need the practice. The hardest part of fishing trout was finding them; even harder was standing still long enough and moving slowly enough to get a stab at them.

Standing over a calm area in the stream, remaining as still as possible, I started thinking about what we had become as a society. We took for granted all that we had. Very few people go hungry unless they are just not willing to put forth any effort. We live in a world of overabundance, which has made us lazy and pitiful.

It was during this momentary trance when my prey appeared, and I began the slow assault on my dinner. Slowly I inched my spear down to the water. He was a nice-sized brown trout, and I could almost taste it cooked over an open fire. I took my time. What else did I have? To win this duel, I would have to be more patient than I had ever dreamed. I was ready, just another inch or two. Then just like that, he was gone. The whole process took at least twenty minutes, and I was still hungry. Now I knew how lions must have felt after tracking and stalking their prey for hours only to walk away with nothing but a growling stomach. I was going to need some practice or a different approach if I was going to give myself a chance to actually catch something. Until then, I'd check around for berries, fruit, nuts, and finish off what I brought.

After missing that trout, I spent some more time pondering the life I had been living P.C. (pre-cancer). I had the illusion that everything I had, everything I knew, was real, when in actuality I had created a false reality. My emphasis on time, money, and position were all illusive creations I could never attain because one step up meant there were ten more to climb. No matter how high I climbed on the ladder, it was never enough. I had created an empty, useless reality. The lifestyles we live, the things we believe in, the things we think we can't live without, none of those were real. It all seems real because we set it up that way so we had a context in which to live. In order for us to feel successful, we needed others not to be. In order to be attractive, we needed others not to be. Someone else had to feel bad so I could feel good. Our society had taught us narcissism was the way to survive. Look out for *numero uno* and *numero uno* only.

All my life I had felt this sense of the illusion, and I had tried to live with the understanding that none of it was real. That was tough at any time. You were constantly being measured and stigmatized, and it was easier to just give in, accept it, and become desensitized to the whole thing. Not here. The very essence of survival was the only thing being played out. My mind was becoming very clear, and as the days went on, my reality would become very clear as well.

Tomorrows here were limited, and as I thought of my plans for attempting to spear a trout the next day, I felt a real sense of urgency and fear. This was no trial, no practice run. There were few second chances. If I was to survive long enough to become what I needed to be before I passed, I had to own that responsibility. We as a culture had become so good at never being wrong, never taking responsibility for our actions that the whole idea of truth was as lost as our ability to conceive it. Think about it. You could lie and always had a reason why you lied. You could be overweight and blame the food manufacturers. You could get divorced, blame your spouse, and know that six months later you could get married again. There was only the reality here, and the truth was I must eat to stay alive. It might take me all day to just get one meal, so patience and focus were things I needed to learn.

At the next attempt I increased my odds. On the end of my stick I tied several smaller sticks to give me a better chance. Upstream I found another brownie trout, and with careful patience I stalked it. I could feel the air upon my skin. I felt every muscle in my body ready to do what they needed to. The water was cold running across my legs, and I could feel the cool air flowing through my lungs. Never had I felt so focused, my mind clear and my body energized. Carefully I moved like I was part of the surroundings. Slowly and with precision, my stick moved closer and closer to the target, and just like that, before I knew it was over, on the end of my pole was not just a fish but a success better than closing a million-dollar deal. I would carry my kill back to Lazarus and eat like a man who was a man.

Thursday

Last night as I cooked and ate my dinner under a starlit sky, it occurred to me that this was one of the most special times in my life. For the first time, I caught and ate my own food. I had eaten some incredible dinners at some of the finest restaurants in the world, but not one of them could compare to that dinner. The thought dawned on me how much food I'd wasted in my life, the times I complained when it wasn't seasoned just right and how I took for granted going to the grocery store and filling up the cart. A sense of pride welled up inside me, and each bite I took brought me closer to where I set out to be.

After dinner, I lay back and watched the fire. Once again it dawned on me how alone I was. This was going to be one of the toughest challenges to mentally overcome. In our society, in what was referred to politely as the civilized world, we had come to depend on people for everything. Other people dictated how much money we could earn, what religion to believe in, how to dress, and how to feel under certain sets of circumstances. Here, there was only the truth, and I was faced with it every moment whether I liked it or not. There was no blaming someone else for my mistakes. There was no manipulating a situation to fit my need. There was no numbing myself in front of a TV screen, and there was no one to talk to.

But that was the whole beauty of it, if you could handle it. That was why I was here, to leave this life like I came, a blank slate. With that thought, I wrote these words:

> There once was a man who dreamed he could fly.
>
> He dreamed that if he believed enough he could take flight.
>
> In his sleep, he flew effortlessly and flew great ships not even known to man.
>
> Years and years went by, and he felt that he no longer desired to crawl on the ground but to lift to the skies … into the heavens.
>
> Now came a trip with his wife to the high bluffs in New Mexico.
>
> One afternoon on a hike to the top, he stared over into the canyons below.
>
> His wife, knowing what was about to happen, smiled as he looked deep into her eyes. "Don't worry," he said. "I will fly." With that, he took a great leap, and as his body fell to the earth below, a great eagle came from him. The eagle danced in the wind and performed magic in the sky. He flew with total abandon. It was a beautiful, loving, free acrobatic show of truth and faith.
>
> After a while, the eagle perched on a tree near his wife and called out as if to say, "I flew!" With a great lift in his wings, he flew out and straight up into the sky, heaving his great wings with a mighty thrust. He flew straight up into the clouds, past the stars, into heaven … to his Father's side, where he sits today.

Last night, with no sleeping pills, no scotch, just a warm glowing fire and the sound of God all around me, I slept. Once again my dreams were vivid and real. I could feel the temperature around me. I could taste and hear everything. And like the other dreams, there was a strange fog that was present. In this dream

I could see how the trees and plants operated. I could see the energy that came off them and how they worked in unison with everything around them to survive. I could see them breathing and taking in water. As I watched, I could see how life worked as it had for millions of years. When I awoke, I had trouble distinguishing between the dream and reality at first. I just know that when I woke up my senses were on level ten, like when someone was being hunted or watched. I think I was experiencing both.

Today would be more like yesterday, locating food and staying alive. I needed to get a stockpile of food for the days to come when I wouldn't be able to hunt or the weather wouldn't permit. From the little I've read in my survival book, if a man had the time and knew where to look, there was plenty to eat in the mountains. I certainly had the time, and I was in the right place, so it was time to get busy.

As I walked, it amazed me how focused I was, not thinking about ten things at once as I usually did. I could not help thinking how life in my circle of friends and acquaintances had become so busy that it was almost impossible to focus on just one thing and do it right. The phone rang nonstop; work pushed you in a hundred different directions; your spouse, pets, friends, and relatives all required time and attention. At the end of the day, you wondered what happened to all your time. Was that how life ended for most of us? Did we look back over our lives and wonder what happened? Was all that chaos really necessary?

It felt so good to be able to focus on just one thing. I could feel my brain becoming very powerful doing it. My vision was becoming clear, like I had never opened my eyes before, and my memory of the books on survival I read in the past was coming to me clearly. There was another unknown sense kicking in because I was feeling more confident in my abilities. Things I had never done before were becoming easier, more natural feeling. Hunting for food was one of those things. I had less fear about the things I ate, and I did it with more purpose. I was beginning to have faith in myself and how I was being led.

The day passed, and with some luck and a lot more practice, I caught six more trout. I had a pretty good sack full of berries and roots and pine nuts and took note of other possible sources of food that I would have to read up on first. Tonight I'd start building a trap for rabbit and other small varmints that would be a welcomed treat on the fire because one thing's for certain: I am going to have to learn how to survive in this place until the cancer kills me.

On my way back today I thought of what a normal day would have been like back home. My days would start at 6:00 a.m. I would put in, on average, a ten-hour day at work and then make the hour drive home. So, with the travel time and the hours at the office, I would have used up twelve hours of my twenty-four-hour day. It would take me another half hour to get my mind off of work, and then I would settle in to numb myself at the TV. If I had the energy, I would go run a few miles and then eat a quick dinner. By then, I would be tired and thinking about bedtime. But then there were the finances to do and talk to Lisa about our schedules. In between all that, I would try to find the time to talk to a few friends on the phone and think about the two-week vacation I had coming.

How did we ever get duped into believing we were supposed to work sixty hours a week and worry about it the rest of the time? How did we allow this to happen? To think that out of fifty-two weeks in a year, I only had two weeks of vacation time for myself. This never made sense to me and still doesn't. We did all this planning and worked our lives away so that someday we could retire and then do all the things we wanted to do. Very few people I knew ever retired and did all the things they wanted to do. Somehow we forgot that living was living now. This moment, this hour, this day, this week, this year!

As I began working on a trap to capture small game, I remembered a book I had read, *Into the Wild,* about a kid who became disillusioned with society and eventually went to live a life in Alaska, away from all the trappings and illusions of this life. He had taken his time getting used to a slim diet and learning all there was to know about surviving in the wilderness. Like many before him, including writers like Thoreau and London, this kid, Cris McCandless, found himself struggling for answers as to why he was here and what the meaning of everything around him was and what was he going to do with his life. He also died in his pursuit. Now that I had time to really think about it, it seemed that just about everybody I had ever known had fought with the same problems. In some capacity, we all seemed to be asking the same questions, whether it was with the career we wanted or why relationships seemed to be so hard or just the general feeling of not knowing what our purpose was. Rich or poor, we all shared the same emotional struggles. Somewhere deep inside we wished for something else.

As I sat back and thought about this struggle, I prayed.

God, as I look back at my life, I see so many wonderful things, and I thank You for all of them, for You have truly blessed me with so much. But God, why was my life and that of so many others such a struggle every day? Why is it that nothing ever seemed right no matter how right it was? God, I look back, and it's like half my life was wasted from all of the worry and confusion and insecurity of what I was doing. God, I have loved You with all of my being. I have prayed my whole life. Was that not enough to take away all the struggle? What are we doing wrong that keeps us in the constant state of disorder?

Just maybe, I wondered . . .

I have chased happiness when it was here all along.

I have searched for peace while it was everywhere I looked.

I have asked for forgiveness when I had already been forgiven, cried for love while I was being loved.

I dreamed of understanding when I knew the truth, looked for strength while carrying a heavy load.

I have asked to be able to forgive when I couldn't remember why, listened for answers to questions that had no answers.

I sought to be heard when all were listening.

I asked to prosper though I was rich.

Sought after success while being rewarded.

Why? Why? Why? Because I am human, limited to the words I think and the words I write.

Friday

In my dreams I was reliving unresolved moments and issues in my past. But it was only moments that were important that I'd missed or didn't recognize. Like when I was too busy at work to listen to Lisa about something that was bothering her, and when I didn't stay for my aunt's funeral because I had to catch a flight to a meeting, and when my sister wrote me a poem for Christmas and I just said thanks without reading it, and when my friend was going through a divorce and I didn't recognize the pain he was going through. And then there was Doug and how I was too caught up in my own problems to help him deal with his. The list went on and on. I think I understood that we got so caught up in everything that we forgot what was important, yet we still knew what was important, and that caused the struggle and conflict.

Along with this morning, as with most, came even more clarity; each night now seemed to have an important message or lesson for me. Each day brought a new meaning, a new challenge. I realized I didn't have to make the same mistakes over and over. I realized I could break the patterns that had kept me in a revolving state of confusion, and I now knew and understood the power that I had over my conditions.

With the sun beginning to shine down upon me, the cancer element hit me hard. As I stoked the fire and readied myself for the day, a prayer came to me. It came from the depths of my soul.

Dear Father, save us one more time. How did we let it get this far? Forgive our stupidity, as we valued today more than the next. Our tears have rained down in shame, yet we ignore the implications of our ways. Our ignorance is more powerful than gold.

We question; we probe; we speculate while we digest the very thing... take in... breathe in. Why is it we don't shout from the highest mountain? No more! We stop!

Years come and pass, and we make it worse with each light.

We continue to pray—treat and prosper at our own expense.

Then when the day is lost, we say it is God's will so we don't have to take responsibility for the sins against ourselves.

Oh God, are we so foul that we are not worth saving? Are we once again at our own mercy?

Forgive us one more time. Send down Your sunbeams and cleanse the foulness from our bodies, each and all, and fill our minds with truth. Give us the strength and the power over ourselves to overtake these weaknesses. Or take away this free will that we have used as a weapon upon ourselves.

I'm so mad at myself, with all the warnings that I have read, printed on every box, reported on the news every night. Warning, these things may cause cancer. Yet I continued, not willing to make some very easy changes in my life to decrease the chances that I would not be in this situation. How could we take such a chance with the most important thing in our lives? We treat our cars better than we treat our bodies. Hospitals all over the world were full of people like me that just ignored what they were doing to their bodies and minds. We knew that stress and anxiety killed, but we lived with it anyway.

Of all the people I've known that had families, that had money, and that had futures, who would make changes because of what I was going through? What changes would they make now? What would they do differently if they knew what their future held for them? If I had known I would be stricken with cancer, would I have believed it and made changes? All the warnings were given through every media source available, and I still ignored them, thinking it wouldn't happen to me. These things happened to someone else. Now I knew that was not true. These things did happen to me. Would the people I knew in my former life—my former work associates, family members, friends—would they make changes because of me? The answer to that was pretty clear. After all, things like this didn't happen to them, and like a dangerous game of Russian roulette, we keep pulling the trigger, hoping the bullet is not in the next chamber.

Today I would push the boundaries of my surroundings. I would also push the boundaries of my mind. There was still the issue of food and whether I could survive this place until the cancer killed me. I would walk north today. I had not been that direction yet, and it looked like the most rugged. My lungs were starting to feel much better, and I was starting to feel some strength in my legs, so I would be able to cover more ground.

As I walked today, I began thinking of one of the reasons I was here. I wanted to be completely aware and in the moment when I passed from this life to the next. I wanted to know the exact instant; I wanted to feel the progression. Was I a fool? Was this some romantic, spiritual thought that I would soon regret as I lay somewhere on this mountain in the most extreme pain, bleeding, foaming at the mouth in some kind of uncontrollable fit? Would I miss the very moment that I had dreamed of, or would I contemplate taking my own life? Which, by the way, I had before, you know.

Cancer could be a horrific death, and even sometimes the morphine didn't even help. I saw that with Doug. How could I believe that I was stronger, different than the millions that had shared the same fate? After all, it was not like I'd been some kind of monk or saint. In a nutshell, I was just a guy who saw his best friend die a terrible death and made the statement that I would never let that happen to me. And now here I was. The only difference between me and Doug was that I had loved God all my life and over the years had become a very spiritual individual. That had changed the way I thought and looked at things, most of which I had kept to myself like so many other things in my life.

Now that I think about it, most of my life had been one big secret. I don't think anybody really knew me. That was my fault. I just never talked about the things that I really thought about because I was afraid that it would sound weird or make me look peculiar. We lived in a culture that was not too accepting of those who talked openly about what was on their hearts or discussed candidly about the things that were bothering them. We didn't talk honestly about love and happiness for fear that people would think we were out there, a bit eccentric.

The complexity of me as a human was more than most people would want to get into, and I really hadn't shared all of me with too many people. Now that I was away from the distractions and the things that allowed me to avoid sharing the real me, I could appreciate how much we had to learn from each other. There were probably many more people that I would have loved to get to know and would have become close to if I had taken the time and made the effort. We had really just stopped caring. There were not too many people who really cared or wanted to know, so what was the purpose? While pondering this latest revelation and new questions, the following thoughts came to my mind:

Don't laugh at me; it hurts.

Will you take a minute to care?

If not, how can I love you?

It's what you want, isn't it?

I think about the same things as you.

I was born.

I will die.

You search for your purpose.

Mine tries to find me.

Our eyes meet every day.

We hear each other at every moment.

Somehow we think it will be tomorrow.

Or was it last week?

Let's not wait until then.

After walking some distance, I descended into a deep valley. There I found a beautiful stream and stopped for a while for some rest and fishing. I started a quick fire and lay back and shut my eyes to listen to the music all around me. It was far better than anything the Rolling Stones had recorded. As I lay there, I became so aware of my body. I could feel each organ as it worked with its intended function, all working in unison and precision. How could anybody believe that somehow over time this incredible, living miracle just created itself? Heart, lungs, kidneys, brain, blood, bones, muscles. As I meditated and concentrated, I focused on each one, looking at it, feeling it, in awe of it. *How did you do this, God? Could it be possible that You gave me the ability to mend and heal my own body? Could that really be true? If so, how?* I lay there and thought about that possibility for a while then slept.

When I woke up and started looking around, a fear overcame me. Where was I? Which way was home, and how did I get here? One wrong decision and I might possibly never find my sanctuary again. What would I do? I would surely die and not the way I wanted. Why hadn't I paid more attention? I knew better. I looked left; I looked right, in front of me, and behind me. Nothing looked right; it just all looked the same.

The fear and anxiety was sapping me of my energy and my breath, and the peace I was becoming accustomed to had turned to panic. I looked around at the mountains, grass, trees, and rocks;

everything looked the same. Just as I was thinking there was no worse feeling than being lost, I heard.

You are never lost; you are just sometimes going in the wrong direction. It's not so much where you are but where you want to be.

When I thought about the statement, I thought about all the times in my life when I'd felt lost, not knowing what to do, which way to turn. Normally after some careful thought, good questions, and sometimes some hard lessons, it became apparent that I was just going in the wrong way. Sometimes life could be like that. We just made the wrong decisions and went the wrong direction. *Life is about course correcting,* I thought. If you had been going down a certain path and it was not working out for you, just change your course.

All the books tell you that panic is the worst thing you could do when you get lost in the woods, that you must remain calm. Just like life. Again, as I thought about it, when I used to panic about something, I would lose the ability to see through the situation. It would be days later when I would look back and wonder why I panicked at all. All that worry had been for nothing.

Never panic until it's time to panic; sometimes you are just where you need to be.

Okay, this was getting scary. *God, is that You really speaking to me? I have never stopped speaking to you. You sometimes just don't listen.*

The voice must have been inside my head, but I knew I heard it with my ears. Was that what it took until we listened, a booming voice from the heavens? How many times do we ignore the very thing we long to hear? Was I just where I needed to be? Had I been in the right place before and just didn't know it? What was here for me? Why did I need to be here?

I made the decision and started up the side of the canyon trying to remember how many I had crossed and from what direction. After two hours, I still didn't see anything that looked familiar and was no closer to figuring out where I was at. This was bad; I could literally walk and climb until I couldn't make it anymore and would probably just go mad.

Sitting there in my panic-stricken state, my head in my hands, I saw to the right of me what looked to be a clay pot of some kind. As I looked it over, I saw others and something that looked like tools of some kind. Had I stumbled on an ancient Indian campground? They were beautiful and so purposeful, and as I touched them, a strange feeling came over me. The wind began to blow, and the sky started changing colors. *I must be losing my mind,* I thought, *or did some of the berries I ate have me hallucinating?*

Looking down on the ground, I saw what looked like an amulet of some kind. It was a beautiful metal piece that had carvings in it that looked like they were filled with gold and some other kind of beautiful stone. It was remarkable, and it had an old leather strap attached to it. It was the most unbelievable thing I had ever seen. As I picked it up and held it in my hands, my head started to get dizzy, and I began to rock back and forth, like in a trance. What was going on? What was happening? Everything around me started to look different, kind of vibrating and out of focus. I shut my eyes to try to clear my head and get a hold of myself, thinking that maybe I was just suffering from panic and fear.

When I opened my eyes, I began to see what looked like a ripple in the water, but it was in the air right in front of me. It started getting closer and divided into two shapes; they weren't quite clear, but as they got closer, they started taking form. They were native Indians, two of them. One was young, and one looked to be very old. Their hair was long and jet-black, and their skin was tanned. They were strong, beautiful, and powerful, and they came closer and sat down beside me. They didn't speak but looked deep into my eyes, and I felt their thoughts. They were telling me to quiet my mind and to believe. After a few minutes, the two of them began to chant and hold amulets up to the sky. The amulets were just like the one I held, so I started to do the same, and they nodded their approval ever so slightly.

Moments later, it was like I was seeing the mountains and the entire area from the sky. I was moving all around like a bird though my body remained on the ground. I saw everything—all the creeks, all the valleys, and my way back home. The whole thing only lasted for a few moments, and then it was over. In an instant, I was back on the ground, still holding my amulet to the sky. They were gone, and everything appeared normal again. It was the most incredible experience of my life, and I sat there for hours just reliving each and every moment.

I must have fallen asleep, and when I awoke, the sun was going down and it was getting cold. I still didn't know what had happened. Was all this just a dream? It all seemed so real. With the little sunlight left, I built a fire and camped with my new friends, staying up the entire night thinking with a great deal of clarity of their lives and how they had lived. I saw the food they ate, where they found it. I listened to their music, felt their laughter, and saw their love. They had a great respect for the environment and each other.

Saturday

When the sun came up this morning, there was no doubt in my mind which way I should go to get back to Lazarus Ledge. I thought back and tried to remember all that I'd seen and felt with my extraordinary visitors. Somehow I knew it was important and that I would need to remember this location. I left with the amulet around my neck and a clear sense of direction, thinking sometimes you were in the right place even though it seemed like the wrong place. The words from above had been right.

Arriving back at the ledge, everything seemed different somehow. I felt certain and believed I now possessed some kind of new purpose, some kind of new knowledge that I hadn't had before. As I looked around at my surroundings, I felt more at home, like I belonged here. Did something really happen to me last night? Did Indian spirits do something to me? Or was it God helping me? Or was it just an exhausted dream?

I spent the rest of the day fortifying my home, cleaning up and doing some general maintenance and repair. I had done a pretty good job, but there was still much to do. So with the limited tools I had, I got busy. Each task I completed reminded me that we must continue in our lives to mend and repair our minds and hearts as well. By midday, I worked up a pretty good sweat, and I didn't know if it was the clear mountain water filled with minerals or just the good, clean diet, but I truly felt good. I don't think I could remember feeling this good in my entire life.

Week Three:

COULD THEY
BE WRONG?

Sunday

I continued exploring and learning more and more about my surroundings and where to find food. My trapping skills had been improving each day, and with each hunt my diet became better as well. It was amazing that I didn't have to gorge myself at every meal if I was eating the right nutrients. We heard all the time that much of the food we ate was mostly depleted of all of the minerals and nutrients that made them good for us, but who could really tell? Truth be known, most of what we ate was just like the rest of our lives, just fillers, and the rest of it was killing us. Even with this knowledge, why did we still continue to pollute our bodies with the stuff we ate and pollute our minds with unproductive, limiting thoughts? It was one of those truths that we just ignored because we didn't want to take responsibility for it.

As I sat out on the top of a canyon wall, I drifted back to the day when the doctor told me I had cancer and was dying. Could he have been wrong? It happened all the time. I mean, I felt great, my body had never felt stronger, my mind had never been clearer, and I had no symptoms. What if I could have been healed? What if it was only a matter of taking a few pills or something and it would have been over? Then I would have never been in the same situation as Doug. But what if down the road more cancer came and I was unable to do what I was doing? Would I have died like Doug?

God, tell me I've done the right thing. This is all so confusing. Like the rest of my life, I'm so unsure of every decision I make. Can't I just once know for sure that I'm doing the right thing? As I closed my eyes, I heard his words again.

You can make a decision that will last a lifetime or one that will only last a minute. There is no answer until you make the decision. Like there is light and dark, there are also two ways to live: the right way and the wrong way. The truth you search for is at hand; you must let go of every- thing to see it first.

As I lay back to think about that for a while, I thought about my life and the lives of others. It was very clear that the quality of life and the direction of your life came down to the decisions that you made on a daily basis. Those decisions dictated how your day went, your week, and your life. They affected every part of your life, emotionally, physically, and spiritually.

Looking back at my life, I began to see each decision I had made and the good and bad consequences of each of them. Day by day each decision shaped and molded my life. The job I had, my health, and my relationships. Every aspect of my life was impacted and determined moment by moment based on how much thought I put into those decisions.

So that was what life was really all about, a decision-making process, and when it came right down to it, those decisions dictated the quality of your life on a daily basis. I reviewed in my head the questions I had asked myself a couple of days ago and the answers I got back and then tied those answers to the decisions that I had made in my life. It became very apparent that I never really asked myself good questions about the decisions I was making. If I had, I probably wouldn't have made some of the ones I did or would have made different ones. It seemed a lot of us did that. We spend very little time and research on major decisions in our lives, and then we spend years trying to make something work that wasn't meant to.

I lay there and thought for hours of all the decisions people made every day that shaped and dictated their lives. Rarely was a thought given to the decisions when making them. If someone had helped me understand the impact of all the decisions that I was making when I was young, how different would my life have been? How much more money would I have had? How much healthier would I have been? How much better would my relationships have been? Would I be dying of cancer? How much more peace would I have experienced? Again, all I could think of was that we all just got so busy trying to deal with all of the decisions that we didn't focus long enough on any one of them, and we certainly didn't want to help anybody else with theirs.

I watched an eagle dance in the sky for hours. It was beautiful. He flew with such faith and total abandonment, living every second, every moment like the world was created just for him. Nothing holding him back—no fear, no stress, no anxiety. With total confidence he trusted every move he made. I wanted to be him right then.

One of the reoccurring dreams I had in my life was that I could fly. In each dream, it was always that I had to know without a doubt that I could do it. I had to believe without a doubt; then and only then could I lift up and start to fly. But every time doubt would creep in. I would come back down to the ground, and I would have to start all over. My thoughts on that had always been that if somehow we could believe something strong enough, we could do anything; we could create anything. We don't do it though, because we are afraid that if we fail it will prove what we don't want to know, that we really don't believe we can. What if I jumped off this cliff? Would I be able to fly?

Monday

Last night I didn't sleep. I spent the night thinking about the possibility that I could live for years. How long could I live with the thought that I might not die and could then decide to go home? What would that do to my family and friends? Would they try to put me in a mental home? Even worse, what if I got home and then got sick and died the kind of death I had been trying to avoid? Was this just denial, and, if so, was it natural? Did everyone who was dying go through this? Because I didn't want to die. But if I was dying, I would want to do it on my own terms, not the way I saw Doug and so many others go.

> When you are confused, look up.
> When you are happy, look up.
> When you are sad, look up.
> When life is good, look up.
> When life is tough, look up.
> When you're thankful, look up.
> When you're not, look up.
> Looking left or right will get you nowhere.
> Looking in front or behind will stagnate you.
> You came in this world looking up,
> And you will leave looking up.

As I lay there this morning, it dawned on me that I had not had sex in quite some time. I'd always had a very strong sex drive. The act of making love with my wife had always been so beautiful, feeling the heat of her body, the passion in her lips, and the forgiveness in her climax. Sex with someone you truly loved was incredible. It was a time when you healed, reconnected, and let go. Making love was as important for the soul as it was for the body, if not more, and how you made love spoke volumes to your mate. It made a statement about how much you loved them, respected them, and wanted them. The course of many relationships could be changed in the bedroom versus the courtroom.

As a boy growing up, and even into manhood, we were taught the most stupid things about sex. We were introduced to pornography that depicted a man with a huge organ and a woman screaming with pleasure. What a way to grow up thinking about one of the most precious parts of our relationship with the opposite sex. My dad never said to me, "Son, loving your wife while in the act of having sex is important; making love is important." In fact, he never told me anything about sex. I just learned from the porn magazines with the rest of my friends. So just like that we stumbled through it for the rest of our lives, not truly understanding how important those physical moments together were. In the beginning, we thought that sex was the first step to having a relationship. We bragged to each other and then, when we married, spent the rest of our time thinking about sex with someone else.

I am thankful that this is one part of my life that seemed to be great. Lovemaking with my wife was all that it could be. I used to take the time in my mind and in my heart to feel the love for her, to mend, to enjoy her, which left us both happy and growing stronger together. I took a great amount of pride in knowing and speaking to my friends about my faithfulness as well. Lisa trusted me when it came to this, and that in turn gave me strength and confidence to continue being faithful. Not just physically but emotionally as well.

When my friends and I used to hang out, I would always take the opportunity to talk about sex and relationships with them and not in the way that they were accustomed. I would talk about the act of making love, not just having sex, and how important that was to happiness, to a person's psyche. I would talk about being faithful and what power that brought to not only the relationship but to them individually as well. I would expound on what romance was and how to go about it. As we talked, all of us learned, and, to my surprise, no one ever wanted to stop talking about the subject. It normally was the first time they had ever had the chance to talk openly about these things, and they were hungry to learn and apply the things that would make them better men and husbands. Most of the talks I had with them were for my own benefit, in that the teacher always learns the most

There were many things that could be difficult in a relationship between a man and a woman, especially in a marriage. All you had to do was sit around with your friends for a while and talk about relationships, and you would quickly understand that in our lives it is one of the biggest struggles we go through on a daily basis. Look at all the divorces. For the most part, we learn about relationships from our parents, and in many cases, we were learning from something that was not working in the first place. That was like learning how to build a plane from the plans for a car. This was one of the most important relationships, if not *the* most important relationship in our lives. It was the thing we needed and wanted the most. Why was it so difficult? God knows there have been enough books written on the topic, not to mention all the TV shows and movies. In my life, it certainly had consumed a fair portion of my time and energy. Thinking back all the way to my earliest years, I could see the impact each relationship had on me. So much wasted time, so much drama I could have lived without. Why?

If I looked back and took all that I have learned and then put it into context with the way I saw life now, here was what I felt:

We don't communicate with each other very well.

We let pride and ego rule our emotions.

We don't let go of the past, forgive.

We get too caught up in everything else.

We stop trusting.

We stop listening.

We stop caring.

We don't spend enough quality time with one another.

We put too many expectations and rules on the relationship.

We forget how important the other person is to us.

We forget to love without reason.

We forget to appreciate and honor each other.

Possibly one of the biggest problems would be that we can't just get over ourselves and focus on what's next. There will always be issues, hurts, and struggles. To get through all the roadblocks, we have we have to learn to focus on what's next, not what happened.

Tuesday

I must have finally drifted off to sleep, and again the dreams surrounded by fog came. I saw thousands of people, men and women in relationships. There were visions of them communicating with one another and the process they went through. I could literally see their energy. It was amazing to see the thoughts and conversations that were going on in each of their minds. It was as if they were trying to win a chess match. "I will say this to him or her so that they will have to say that. I will do this to show them what will happen if they do that. I will prove to them why they are wrong."

It was a mess. The very thing that started the argument or situation was not even an issue to them anymore. The past was brought into the situation, issues and hurts from months and years back. Soon, no one knew what they were fighting about, except that they wanted the other person to stop, to give in, and to acknowledge that they were right. Winning was everything. By the time they were done fighting, new damage had been done, which was worse than the original problem, and then they had to deal with that too.

I grew up thinking that I, as the man, always had to be right. I had to be right so that I could prove to my significant other that I was strong, I was powerful. That way she would respect me. I, after all, was the man. If I gave up the superiority and power, where would I stand? For most of my life, that led to control issues that I denied. Lisa would always shake her head in disbelief. And for years, I continued to push my power around like it was a sword. It cut, stabbed, and ripped. It was not until years later that I realized was all wrong, so very wrong.

Why do we let pride and ego get in the way of happiness? Why can't we just stop and say, "I love you, and I don't care who is right or wrong. I'm sorry; please forgive me when I fail. Let me kiss you, love you, and hold you."

In a day or two, we don't even remember what happened anyway. Why can't we just make good decisions to make our lives better instead of making our lives worse? Why do we continue with the same patterns? No one likes or wants to deal with the aftermath of arguments or disagreements. It's easier to just realize no one has to be right or wrong; there doesn't have to be a winner. It's better to be wrong sometimes than very right and very alone. As the dream went on, there were couples that seemed to make it happen the way it should. They valued each other and their relationship more than themselves. They were willing to let go of their pride and ego. They comforted each other and let go of the issue at hand. They forgave each other. They didn't play word games. The words they did use were used to encourage, to build up, to comfort, to heal. The energy between them was beautiful even in the heat of battle. They seemed to know that no matter what had happened they could get through it without hurting each other. Within minutes, they were holding each other, licking their wounds together, moving on; they focused on what was next. They focused on their words.

Words are the most powerful thing we possess:

They can change lives.

They can create love or start wars;

They can heal or destroy.

They can bring peace or bring malice.

All things that we know have their origins from the spoken word. This has never changed and never will. The pyramids were built with a command; the lover is revealed with his pleas, the liar with his tongue. The song cannot be heard without the words, and the rivers and mountains could not have been named without verbal expression.

If we know that words are so powerful, then how is it? We choose to use them in some of the most awful ways. As I lay there and thought about how I had used my words throughout my life, it became clear that my life and the life of others could have been dramatically different if I could have only understood what had just been revealed to me. How many marriages and relationships could not only be saved but thrive if different words would have been said? On a daily basis, how many times could we build up, encourage, comfort, and strengthen? What stops us from using words in the way they were intended to be used? Could it be that we have too much shame and guilt in our own lives that we are afraid that we will look like a phony or a hypocrite? It's hard to encourage someone else when all you talk about is negativity. It's hard to preach love and forgiveness if you are filled with anger and bitterness.

Speak the truth, my lover, with intent.

Come from your mind where you are confused and broken.

Let the words come forth out loud that will free you,

Spoken words of forgiveness, love and greatness, responsibility.

You have too long been a prisoner of your fear of being exposed.

Your greatest day has yet to come, least it be this one, if you choose.

Speak the words out loud that will change your reality.

Those unspoken words are your salvation; they are the key to your transformation from darkness to light.

And God said.

As the sun came up this morning, I looked around at all the beauty and again was feeling quite sexual. Some of the things I saw in that dream were very arousing. In the past, I would have just taken care of that in the usual physical way, mindlessly. But this time the arousal came with a great feeling of love. I took my time and loved myself while in the act with myself, and it was beautiful from the heart. The loving of myself in that way left me feeling high. I longed to be with my wife to share this sensation again.

Today I continued the process of fortifying and making my abode a little more comfortable. It started with continuing work on my bed. I took a look in my survival book but found nothing helpful. I guess they never counted on anybody staying in the wilderness as long as I. As I began gathering the needed materials, I just couldn't get out of my mind the one big question: what if the doctor was wrong?

What if there comes a day when I know that I'm not going to die? What will I do? How will I explain what I've done, where I've been? How will my life change knowing what I know now? I know this one thing for sure: if given another chance, I will live life in a totally different way. I will see life for what it is: the truth. No more living an illusion of what it was supposed to be based on what others wanted me to think, do, or feel. I would talk to people about what I have experienced and what I know. I would help people see and think about things differently. I will change my diet and take good care of my body. I will take the time to truly appreciate and love the people in my life. I will care. There are so many things I will do. I truly will.

For now, I believe I'm in the right place doing the right thing. I will live the rest of my days in love with the life I have left. I will reach out to God and remove all the obstacles that separate me from him, the veil, and obstacles like me. I will spend my last moments aware of the process of leaving this life and passing to the next. That is the reason I'm here in the mountains in the first place. To find the peace and tranquility, to find answers, to die the way I want.

As I continued focusing on the work at hand, I admired the dirt and scratches on my hands. Maybe it's something that's wired into us that we are supposed to use our hands in labor. In a world where everything is pre-built or you pay someone to do it for you, we don't get a chance to exercise that piece of our brain or bodies anymore. We stare into computers, talk on phones, and use remote controls. I used to look at construction guys and think that the only reason they were doing that job was because they couldn't do anything else, because they didn't have an education. Now I thought maybe I was wrong. Maybe they did it because they liked it.

The day progressed, and I was almost finished with what would now be my new bed. It had four legs and slats that ran the length of the supporting rails, made of flexible pine tree limbs. Not too shabby, and it would get me off the ground. I tried it out and took a long nap. When I awoke, my friend Doug was heavy on my mind. I never felt closer to him even when he was alive. Where was he now? Was he guiding me, helping me?

Doug was a great guy, living a good life. He was a lot like me. There was something in him that yearned for more than just a life of confusion and struggles. He often talked about cleaning up his life and living a more purposeful existence. Doug and I used to talk for hours about life and God, trying to figure out how to escape this life that we had created that was not what we wanted after all. We would joke about starting a company where we worked for ourselves and took time to go fishing and mountain biking. As much as we loved being together, as time went on, we just never could find the time to do the things we liked to do. We would try. We would get out the calendar and try to put something in ink, but somehow something would always come up and one of us would have to cancel.

Those last days seeing him in that condition really did hurt me. I would beat myself up for all the lost time. All the things we planned to do but didn't. I would sit by his bed and wish I could do it all over again. How many of us still do that with people we have lost? We painfully go through that process, and then after just a few days we continue doing the same thing with the ones that we still have. We just let everything else become more important than each other.

There was a crisp breeze in the air, so I built a fire and made some tea from pine needles and wild flowers. The rain had come in, and the air was cold. These were the loneliest times, when I couldn't see very far and everything just closed in around me. There was no life around to watch and no stars to stare up at. It was depressing.

I had started making some wrist bracelets a few days before out of some kind of bush that had a really cool bark. So I huddled down by the fire with my tea and continued. Again, I loved the process of creating things with my hands. I had always been creative but never really did anything with it, just a few drawings that normally ended up in the trash. Now with nothing but time, I was enjoying the process. The deer hide that I had dragged up for bedding worked equally as good for forearm covers. I cut them into straps that would fit over my hands and over my arms. This would become good protection when going through heavy brush that had a lot of thorny vines. Not to mention they made me feel dangerous. As the rain came down, I covered up with the elk hides I had been collecting and had a conversation with Doug.

"My friend, I miss you. I often wonder where you are and what it might be like where you are. What do you know now that you could tell me? Please, if you can help me, show me what to do with this situation. I'm scared, and I miss my family desperately. Can you cure me, or is there a way I can cure myself? Is God everything we had talked about? Doug, I have so many questions. Please come to me if you can. Guide and protect me if you can."

Wednesday

As the days proceeded, it was becoming clear that writers like Thoreau and others like him were not quite so clear when discussing the trials you would go through living a life like this. It was emotionally challenging. As much as I tried to stay busy, there was so much downtime. I took advantage of most of this time to pray and meditate. Often for hours I would pray myself into a state of ecstasy. It would feel as if God was expressing himself through me. There were times that I felt that I could just lift off and fly. My prayers were so intense that I could not even explain them back to myself. Through my mediations and prayers, I experienced a state of unbelievable peace. I spent many hours exploring my body, mind, and soul.

I longed for my wife, family, and friends. Even as I tried not to dwell on the thoughts of them, it was nearly impossible. I could see all of them. I could see Lisa, whom I missed with my whole being. I could see my three wonderful sisters, who had been so instrumental in my life, each one of them so very special. Debbie, Karen, and Pam basically raised me. I was very close to them and felt very privileged to have such a loving family. Would they ever forgive me for what I had done? Would they understand? Could anyone possibly ever understand the decision I made?

Even with all the spiritual progress I felt I had made, missing Lisa and my family and all that was happening to me was getting me down. The old demons came to haunt, and I soon slipped into deep depression. Not that I didn't think this would happen. I just didn't think it would be that bad, especially after all I had learned.

So many people I know suffer from some kind of depression. Most of them take Prozac or some other anti-depressant or drown themselves in some other mind-altering method. They all are desperately trying to feel like they know they should. The medical companies have seized this opportunity like they always do, to make us all believe this is purely a medical condition. I don't buy it! Depression is the cumulative effect of not taking responsibility for our emotions and our actions caused from those emotions. It is our soul and spirit at war with the human side of us, telling us to make changes; it's a character disorder, a disorder of responsibility.

Just like everything, over time there is just too much to deal with, and we turn to a quick fix to make us feel better and take our minds and hearts off the issues. Food, alcohol, chemicals, and sex are just a few. Then before we know it, we have addictions to deal with. Do I even know anyone without some kind of addiction? So day after day, we try to escape; day after day, we add to the problem; day after day, we slip further behind until we find ourselves with a mountain that is too tall to climb. In our weakness, we allow the things that are not good for us to take hold; then we punish ourselves.

I didn't leave the ledge much, and I had lost my desire to gather food. For the most part, I just lay around and got lost in being depressed.

Thursday

I started praying with intent. I made myself get up and start fishing and trapping. I jumped in the stream, which was extremely cold, and stayed until I was screaming. I would not let depression and self-pity be the outcome after all I had done. I would see this negativity for what it was, the remnants of old thinking, thoughts that were still hanging on from the illusion of life. The old life said I was supposed to be like this, feel like this, die like this. Then I remembered one of the first things I heard from the voice of my maker. *Allen, you are a spiritual being living a human existence.* I had to find that spirit. I had to remember that life was about evolving. That is why we are all here—to evolve, not to go backwards or be stagnant in our lives but to become what we were meant to be, to fly like an eagle over the desiccated landscape.

I had to cleanse all negative thoughts from my body and mind. Negative thoughts create energy that saps the body of the strength it needs to be healthy and strong. Looking up at the peak of the mountain, I started for it and began climbing. I started climbing as fast as I could. My pace and my thoughts kept me from paying attention to the burning in my lungs or the weakness in my legs. Four hours later I reached the top. Throwing my arms out wide, my head back, I yelled at the top of my lungs, "I will not quit! I will not die in vain! I will not be just a human!"

Sitting there on the top of that mountain, I surrendered myself to God again. It seemed to me that I should be running out of opportunities, but God always took me back when I had fallen short in trusting him. In that moment, I felt it deep within my soul. All that I had ever been, all that I was now, and all that I was going to be was given to God. I'm glad there was no one around to see me as I pounded my chest in a show of strength and then went down on my knees. Now that I was able to put feelings with my thoughts, I needed to turn those same feelings and thoughts into action. I liked how that sounded. The universe was speaking to me, telling me to bring down the walls.

The rain started coming down hard, harder than I had seen since I'd been here. That made it impossible for me to trek back down. I could barely see, and everything had become very slick. One bad decision or wrong move up here and you could end up dead or worse, severely hurt. So I stayed.

It would be a long night. I huddled up under a rock overhang. There was very little space, and the rain still managed to come in. I must have looked pitiful, in the fetal position, wet and cold. This, though, would be a part of the cleansing process that I needed. I knew I would not sleep, so I made the decision to meditate my way through this predicament.

Father, You have led me to every place in my life. I know I'm here for a reason, and I think I know what it is. Open my heart, my mind, my soul, and let me feel Your presence. Help me to overcome these weaknesses; help me to find the spirit that You put in me, my strength, my power.

As the rain completely soaked me, I felt nothing, just the air coming in and out of my lungs. The sound of the rain and the smell of the night air was like a drug. I quickly slipped into a beautiful trance. All week I had felt that maybe I had made a mistake or maybe the doctors had made a mistake, maybe everything was a mistake.

I called out to Doug. "I know you're with me right now. Come to my mind, my heart, and show me where to go. I know the veil that separates us is no longer there. I know you can hear me; help me to hear you."

My mind drifted back to the night the Indians were with me. Their power was still with me. I again saw and felt the warmth of the glowing fire we sat in front of that night, the comfort of their presence around me. The smoke from their fire engulfed me, and then Doug was there. As always, he had a big smile on his face, and he radiated love and peace.

He spoke to me, saying, "Allen, you are where you should be. Have faith, and trust your heart. You are being watched over. Stop questioning and doubting."

"Doug, I have so many questions; are you really here?"

"Allen, have faith and trust."

"Doug," I was pleading with him, "did I do the right thing? Will what I'm doing put me in the place I want to be? Will I die from this cancer? Will I survive? Should I have pulled the plug when you asked me? Did you know when you passed from this life to the other? What was it like?"

Doug looked at me with such tenderness and an indescribable love. "To the extent that you believe, these questions are going to be answered. There is no wrong or right, only the outcome that you create. It's not for me to answer these questions but for you to reveal for yourself, within yourself. What you are creating will soon become reality and the questions you are asking answered. Take care, my friend. I love you."

As quickly as he had come, he was gone. It made me sad to see him go, but I had things to ponder, things he had revealed to me that I already knew but was waiting for spiritual affirmation. I had always believed that we create our own reality. Whether we are happy, sad, rich or poor, healthy or sick, we create our relationships and how we think, feel. Doug had confirmed what I was thinking, what I believed. I created this moment, this place. If this was true, then a lot of the places in which we put ourselves are not only by our choice but for a reason. This puts a whole new light on the decision-making process that we go through on a daily basis. We must learn to make decisions that put us in the right places for the right reasons.

All these years I had put off getting true understanding of what my real relationship with God was, always waiting for the moment when the time was right. I had, as I said, always considered myself a spiritual person, but I was not a committed spiritual being. If I could tell the world one thing right now, it would be this: Don't wait for the moment to come. Take pleasure in every moment as it comes because you just don't know what the next moment will be. Get down on your knees, look up to the heavens, shut the world out, and go to God. As I fell to my knees, I heard these words:

Allen, be aware of your life and your mind together right now, not just when you are hurting or sad or at the threshold of death. You have gone to the extreme to find Me. You could have found Me years ago, but I'm glad you are here now, with Me, in this place. I am pleased with you and what you are becoming. The words were spoken to and heard by my heart, soul, and spirit.

As I thought about these words, I thought about all the many times in my life I had procrastinated. I waited to get healthy, waited to read a book, waited to work on my finances, waited to change jobs. When I looked back, it appeared I'd spent most of my life in waiting mode, like a plane hovering, waiting to land.

That is probably true with most of us. We wait to go see a family member that we haven't seen in years. We say next week we'll quit smoking. We wait till a new year begins and make resolutions that this year we're going to do things differently. What God was telling me was don't wait; choose now!

Week Four:

RAIN/REFLECTING BACK ON LIFE

Friday

This morning as the sun came up and shone into my eyes, I realized once again that something very powerful was happening. The voices, the dreams, the visits from Doug, the conversations with God, and how His words were becoming more vivid and real in my life were creating a powerful change in me. Doug had said I was in the right place. He told me that to the extent that I believed, the questions I was asking would be answered. I had to trust, believe, have faith that all this was real and was leading me to something bigger than I could ever imagine.

With the sun on my body and the wind blowing across my face, I thought about faith and belief. What did I really believe in? What did I really have faith in? I read somewhere that man is at his finest when he truly believes in something, when his faith is the strongest. We have a really hard time believing and having faith in anything because we are so afraid we will be let down, or worse yet, we are afraid of being taken advantage of. With everything we see happening in politics, relationships, religion, and everything else in our lives, it's tough, but that's when we become the strongest. We find power in our beliefs, and to believe is to have faith. No man is more powerful than the one who has faith and believes. That's when you experience your finest moments. That's when you have control over your limiting thoughts and become focused.

In the days to come, I will be tested in my faith and believe in many ways I'm sure. I know I'm not quite there yet, but like the sword that is forged out of cold steel, I hope to become what I never was but know that I can be.

All week it rained day and night. All I could do was sit around and watch it. I should have been bored, but I wasn't. All my life I'd wondered what it would be like just to do nothing for a week. I mean nothing, just sleep, study a rock for a couple of hours, or whatever. I felt great peace just staring into the fire for hours at a time.

I'd often wondered what the human mind could do if one had enough time, like, say, a Buddhist monk. I had meditated most of my life but always felt like there was something else I was missing. I always seemed to lose the focus when I got to a certain point. There were just very few opportunities to find a time when there were no phones ringing, doorbells chiming, or dogs barking, and my mind was always just so consumed with everything that was going on.

The contemplation of freedom, free heart, free mind, and free conscience was something I'd pondered for years. Is there really such thing as total freedom? Were the monks in Tibet really free? Did they not feel some kind of pull from their idea of society? How many times had I felt like moving to Tibet and giving up everything I knew to live that kind of life?

Can we truly live a life in society that allows us to experience this state without ridicule, or is it just a romantic thought? There are many books out there about people who have tried it to some degree. I wonder if they found what they were looking for. When most of the people in my circle of friends think of freedom, they think about time and money. If we only had enough money we would be free, if we only had more time. But most of the people I know who have money and time aren't free. They still struggle with the same issues I do.

I think the answer may be in the process of living a life knowing what freedom is. Freedom is an attitude, a detachment from the thoughts that keep us from thinking at a higher level. That process would include letting go. Letting go of the past, letting go of ego and pride, letting go of anxiety and stress, letting go of everything that keeps you out of the here and now. We all hold on to everything so tightly that we literally accumulate a prison for ourselves. We hold on to things that happened years ago, things that happened last month, last week, yesterday. How can we be free if the prison we live in is of our own doing? I can think back and remember so many people telling me the reason that their lives are like they are is because of what happened to them as a child or what happened in a past relationship. Why is it they, we, feel such a need to hold on to the past and all the other things that keep us from being free?

So if the prison we live in is our own making, no one else can let us out. We must do it ourselves; it is up to us. I know a lot of us look for someone else to have the key to let us out. We look to our parents, our spouses, and our preachers. Then when they can't, we resent them for it. But if you desire to have a different life other than the one you have, you must do your part. You must take the steps necessary to be reborn.

I know from experience, and from friends, that in almost every argument references to what they did or did not do months and years before seem to be an issue. Why focus on what was when instead you can focus on what can be? We waste so much time and

ON THE LEDGE OF LIFE

energy holding on to what was that we can't live today. *If you want to live today, forget yesterday.*

If living in days gone by is not bad enough, most of us spend the rest of our time thinking about the future. We let our minds get consumed with what can happen, or will happen, which, if we look back, most of what we spent our time worrying about never happened. So in a nutshell, there it is. We are consumed by worries about ancient times and the future. We can't just enjoy this moment in life.

An increasing number of doctors tell us that possibly half of all the disease and illnesses that they see are from feelings and thoughts that people have literally allowed to make them sick.

I decided to take inventory of my own life. Are these the things that have made me sick with cancer? The truth is I have lived in a prison of fear and guilt, the past and future. Things I've done that I haven't let go of. Thinking back to my childhood, I grew up very confused about my life and who I was. My mother had a tough life, married to an alcoholic who worked only when he wasn't on a drinking binge. We moved around a lot and had very little. I remembered as I got a little older I would make up excuses to tell my friends about our lifestyle. I was always embarrassed and tended to hang around others who had similar situations. These were kids like me, and we were always getting in trouble. When I was about twelve, I learned the man I'd always thought was my father wasn't. This new man standing in front of me, whom I was meeting for the first time, was my father. You want to think about what that did to me? It was a big secret that everybody knew about but me. Then he died a few years later.

So I grew up feeling I was less than others. I envied other kids and families that seemed stable. When the questions came, I always lied or moved on to other kids who didn't ask "normal" questions. I'd carried that stigma with me my entire life, and I knew that my sisters did the same. I don't blame my mother. I'm sure she did the best she could. But why did I allow that to affect my life so many years later?

It really had nothing to do with today. How much time did I lose holding on to unconscious thoughts and emotional pains that had nothing to do with the quality of my life now?

The insecurity that I'd felt my whole life was about things that happened long ago or things that I was afraid might happen in the future. No one made me feel this way except myself. In fact, I never really talked to anyone about any of it. As I sat there staring into the fire, I let go of it all. Tears poured down my face like the rain coming down outside. I forgave my mother, and I forgave myself.

The wounds that we carry around are one of the ways we keep ourselves from living in the now. If we want to truly live, we must forgive, forget, and move on. Each of us must get real with ourselves and quit using all those memories as excuses for not experiencing the greatest moments in life, for keeping us from being fully alive.

For the next couple of days, I looked at everything that I still held on to, and I did the same thing I did with my mother. I let them go. I saw them for what they were, old memories, and I cried them out. I made the decision that with the days I had left they would no longer be a part of me and that they had no power over me.

That night I slept again like never before, and then shortly after waking, I went back to sleep and slept another four hours. It was like my body and mind were thanking me for ridding myself of all the trash that'd been keeping me from capturing pure, restful sleep. When I was awake, I simply rested. I must have been exhausted from life. All the guilt for things I'd done, all the pain, all the wounds I had carried around, all the fear that I was going to be found out was pouring out in sheets. I no longer even had to try to find them; they found me. After hours of my soul releasing all that it could, I would sleep some more. I slept. I rested. I slept and meditated. I slept and prayed. I let go of myself. I was finding my soul.

Why hadn't I done this many years ago? How much differ-ent would life have been if I had? How much more would I have laughed? How much more would I have loved? How much better would my relationships have been? How much more peace would I have had? How different would my life have been? And would I still have had cancer?

As I continued meditating, I gained focus. There were times I felt that I could fly. There were times I could see the future. There were times I experienced God thoughts. My mind was clear, my heart was free, and I felt in love with life and felt life was in love with me. I saw the cancer inside of me, and I focused great amounts of energy on it, allowing God to express himself through me. I prayed differently now with confidence, without doubt, with truth and belief.

In the midst of all that was happening to me, I started drawing a picture of my life on the rock wall beside me. The sticks from the fire worked well as charcoal pencils. Just like the cave dwellers from thousands of years ago, I depicted my life. Would this make any sense to those who might someday find it? What would they see? What would they think? It didn't really matter; it was really just for me.

That night there was a break in the rain, and the clouds opened up and let the heavens be revealed. I stared up and contemplated eternity. I let my mind go and started traveling up through space, past the moon and the stars, stopping to admire the beauty of each of them. Looking back occasionally at the planet I called home, I continued. What would I see? How far would I go? Could I get back home? It was all very scary, this great unknown. As I went faster and faster through space and time, there came a point when I was not just traveling but becoming. I was traveling from one point to another in just a thought, millions of miles in between, and then lifetimes in between. This feeling was unbelievably beautiful. I was no longer in a body. I was thought, an energy, a presence.

There was no memory of my past life, just an awareness of the moment. As I continued, for what seemed like billions and billions of light-years, the dark turned to light, the most beautiful, soft, loving light I had ever seen or felt. It was all around me; I was floating in it, like in water. I could just be in it, around it, part of it. It was incredible. Where was I? Could this be heaven? There was no noise; there were no seams, no beginning, no end or anything to touch, just light that engulfed me.

Then my name was spoken. Not in a way I had ever heard it, not in a language I had ever heard, not in a tone or sound that I had ever heard, but it made sense to me. It was powerful in every sense of the word. Not only did I hear it, but I felt it; it was me and I was it. Then things starting appearing all around me. They were not things I recognized, like a house or a tree, more like something that was made of only a vibrating energy. I was somehow in another existence.

It was a civilization of some kind. I couldn't make out faces or bodies, but they were alive; they were real. I could seen them interacting with one another and communicating. I could see the energy that they were giving to each other. The more they communicated, the more they lit up. They were trying to show me something. The feeling was that of pure love. Love as if I were deaf and blind. They were also showing me how to communicate without fear, guilt, and agendas. I felt like they cared about me deeply, so very deeply. It felt like they were giving me something important, a new way of thinking, feeling, experiencing. *What is all this? Did I die in the process of coming here? Is this the life after death?* I thought.

I wanted more. I needed more. But the more I thought about what I wanted from them, the more they stepped away. Then I realized what they were doing, what they meant. Their message to me was not to want and need more but to enjoy what I have and to give more. Be happy just being. As I thought about it, life was kind of like that. We convince ourselves we need more from the people around us, and the more we ask, the more we demand, the farther they step back. We forget to be happy with just what we have with them, who they are, and what they are. We just continue to want more no matter how much we have. What they were showing me was not to take but give more. That's how you create the energy of life.

After what seemed like a lifetime, I became aware I was back in my being, sitting in Lazarus Ledge and staring up at the sky. I didn't remember when or how I got back, and I couldn't remember when I left. I just sat there looking around as if someone could explain it to me. As I looked down at the skin on my arms, it appeared to be glowing and was sensitive to the touch. Everything around me seemed so clear; all the colors were intense and alive.

The sky was no longer clear but heavy with rainclouds again. As I got the fire going and made some pine needle tea, I tried to grasp what had happened. It was too much for me to understand, but I knew that somehow, whatever happened, I was different. I saw things differently and thought differently. I'm not sure where I was at or what it was I saw, but it was the closest thing to heaven that I could imagine.

That day as the rain continued I made more bracelets out of some kind of vine and rawhide from the deer skins I had found. At first, they were very crude, but with a little practice they started coming together. From there I made some rings and necklaces. My mind was so free. I had a nice warm fire, the scent of the mountains, and the rain. Like in the days and nights before, I slept. My dreams continued to be very vivid. At one point during the afternoon, I really didn't know if I was awake or dreaming.

I continued to reflect back on my life and how so many things could have been different. Did I really know my wife and family? Sometimes I thought I did, but how much time did I spend really trying to understand their dreams and aspirations, their troubles and problems? Now that truth was all I had, the reality had become clear to me.

I think we are capable of such love and understanding, but rarely do we ever take the time to explore what is most beautiful in our lives, the people around us. We are so used to skimming over everything so we can get to the next topic. Even in conversations hardly anyone can get their story finished before someone is talking over them or interrupting. Instead of listening, we are already thinking of what we are going to say next. To truly listen without forming opinions and rebuttal is such a magnificent gift to give someone. How I wished I would have taken more time to really get to know the people around me. I wished I had learned to shut up and listen, to really understand them, to feel them. I wished I had spent more time just truly knowing them by hearing them.

You need to know others, to feel them, to experience them. Did I really know my best friend, Doug? Did I really know his fears and his desires? I should have asked my wife more important questions. I should have asked her what was going on in her mind, her heart, and what her dreams were instead of how her day was going. There were times that I felt we had deep conversations, mostly on the road trips we took. But I'm pretty sure I never sat down with her face-to-face and really talked about her, to her, with her. What a shame; how much I must have missed out on. If only I could do it all over again.

Then there was my own family, my mother and my three sisters. How much did I really know about them? What about their lost dreams? What about what love meant to them? Did I ever ask them what the meaning of life was to them? The fact is that over time I talked to them very little, and when I did, it was just to get the Cliff's Notes version of what was going on. I treated my contact with them like a duty, a responsibility as part of the family, but never as an opportunity in which I delighted.

None of them really knew how I thought and felt either. They didn't know my fears and what I really thought about life. There was never any conversation that would have uncovered the real me. They just saw what was on the surface, just like what I knew about them. And these were the people closest to me in my life.

We really should take the time to know the people in our lives on a deeper level. How much richer would our own lives be if we did? How much more could we love people? Would there be as many divorces? As much hate? Maybe if we took the time to genuinely understand the people around us there wouldn't be so many arguments and disagreements. What could our conversations be like? What if we focused more on strengthening, supporting, and building up the people around us? What if conversations centered around helping each other to live incredible, abundant, joyous lives? We all can make a difference in each other's lives. Simple words of encouragement and support can change lives.

So here was the truth. My life, like so many others, was really only about me, my wants, my needs, my troubles and problems. How many times when I was talking to friends about life issues did I just agree and pile on? When I could have taken a different path, I could have changed the course of the conversation to one that was empowering. I could have been a positive influence and created hope. I could have spoken words of support, a course correction. I could have spoken the truth!

To really know yourself, you have to be dedicated to the truth, a life of never ending dedication to self-examination. You have to shine that flashlight into the deep, dark secrets of your mind. You have to expose all of those dirty little hidden truths that shackle and hold you back from becoming your highest self. You have to bring them out and see them in the light of truth, revealing them to the world so that you have nothing to hide any longer, transparency.

As I thought about conversations I had in the past, it dawned on me that we are mostly poor communicators. We talk to each other, and we have things on our minds, but rarely does it come out the same as we are thinking. It somehow gets lost in the translation. In my conversations with Lisa and family, I would find myself thinking one thing and saying another, and when the person I was talking to didn't react just like I wanted them to, I became frustrated or angry.

We assume people are supposed to read our minds. If you asked someone to pick up that rock and put it over there and you weren't clear where there was, the result would probably not be what you expected or wanted. With the information you gave them, it could be any rock and anywhere around the area you indicated. The right way to decrease frustration would be to say pick up the gray rock by your left hand and put it next to the trunk of that tree on the right side. How much easier would our lives be if we would simply communicate better, say what we mean, and mean what we say? What if we were clear about what we wanted or expected and didn't leave translation up to assumption? What if we communicated like the vision I had in my dream, where we actually gave more than we took?

The worst arguments Lisa and I ever had would always be because she was never clear to me what she wanted or I knew she was not really saying what she was thinking, and it would drive me crazy because I knew it would come out later and I would have to deal with it all over again. And the truth is, I probably wasn't clear as well. We treat our conversations like a game, like pieces to a puzzle. A riddle that none of us has the desire or patience to figure out.

We also let emotions and fear drive most of our communication. Our ego gains strength, and then we really get into trouble. We do this with our kids, people at work, and with ourselves. We cause half the frustrations we go through in life. In the end, most people want to know what you expect from them; they want to get it right. We all want to please the people around us. But for the most part, it is impossible because we are never really clear about want we want in the first place. We then end up guessing about what we want from each other. I learned my lesson the hard way a few times, when I would tell Lisa, "Let's leave to go to dinner around seven." Around seven to Lisa could be almost eight. How many times did I get us in a bad way by not being clear? I started learning to be very clear: "We are walking out the door at seven." Then I wasn't sitting there waiting for her and getting mad, a prelude to a ruined evening.

By the same token, we don't communicate with ourselves any better. We don't really understand what we expect from ourselves, what we really want. I know that for years I was sending myself mixed messages. I never made a statement about what I expected from myself or my life. Just think of all the conversations that go on in our minds. If all the other people in our lives don't confuse us enough, we ourselves add confusion to it. I had lost so many hours and days to poor communication in my life, and I had created so many of the issues. It all made so much more since now; it was so much clearer. I had spent too much time trying to be heard instead of trying to listen.

It was raining, so I took off all my clothes and sat on a rock. I let the rain run over my naked body, trying to feel each raindrop upon my skin. I stared up in the sky and tried to find a raindrop at its highest point and follow it down. How do we miss such simple things that bring our minds and souls such peace? Instead of wondering how a tree gets the water up to the top branches and leaves, we think about how the rain is ruining the chance of golf the next day. Instead of staring at the beauty of someone's eyes, we wonder where they get their hair cut. Instead of thinking of how our heart beats, we wonder about the clothes we have on.

Look into my eyes; see what I truly am.

Touch me; feel what I truly am.

Look past what life has taught me to be; understand who I truly am.

Listen to my words, and hear what I truly am.

Walk with me and go the direction I am.

Stick your finger in my eye.

Spit upon my face.

Curse my name.

Take what I have.

Leave me to die.

And then you will see what I truly can become.

As I sat there with the rain falling down all around me and on me, I thought about my brain and the difference between it and my soul. You know, we all talk about the soul, but how many of us have tried to find it, become connected to it, tried to feel it, be it? We seem quite content in just believing it exists. We walk around thinking that we are what we think. As I sat there with the rain running down my body, I tried to shut down my brain, hoping I could experience my soul, find it, know it. What would it be like?

There are two parts to us. There is the human, man and woman, and there is the soul and spirit. The soul-spirit is the truth. It is what we came here with. It is what God gave us and is our real connection to life. The human side is manufactured. It is the lie; we created it. It is what we have created, taught, and what we have learned. The conflict in life is between the two, the soul-spirit and the human, man/woman. The soul and spirit urges us to see past the experience that we have created and look inwards toward our heart where God speaks the truth to us.

Maybe when I was talking about getting to really know people, that's what I was talking about, getting to know and connecting with something other than the words that come from their mouths, something much deeper, their true existence, what makes them special, the identity that God gave each of us.

As I shut down all my thoughts, I started to concentrate on my body, the air that I was breathing, my heartbeat, the sensation on my skin from the rain, the blood coursing through my veins. I felt my own energy. All at once, I wasn't me anymore. I wasn't my body; there was no attachment. I'm not sure what I was. It was a feeling. I felt like I was as big as the universe, like there were no boundaries. There were no memories in it, and there were no sensations, yet it was not empty. I had no connection to anything except God. I wasn't sure where I was. Was I still on the mountain or somewhere else? It was like being naked in a room with a complete stranger. I was totally exposed. It's not like I could speak to it. I was it, in all my glory. The awareness of me was literally one of the most beautiful things I'd ever experienced, and that's the only way I could describe it. It was me being my soul, and I saw how important my soul really was. It was the only one of its kind, and there would never be another like it.

Think about it; how incredible are you? The words you can put together, the thoughts you can think, the love you can give and receive. We just seem to forget how beautiful and flawlessly created we are, how important we are. We forget about the identity that God gave us. The guilt of the selfishness that we unconsciously hold on to doesn't allow us to see the real greatness in ourselves; we feel shame in our souls. How extraordinary can you be if you only care about yourself? The true power in life presents itself when your life no longer is about you!

Sometime later I was back in my body. It must have been several hours later. My body was cold and stiff, so I dried off and put more wood on the fire. As I lay there by the fire, I wondered what my life would have been like if I had spent more time knowing and loving the real me. What would it have been like if I had tried to see and experience the souls of others instead of just accepting the superficiality of day-to-day encounters? I think I might have come close when I really focused on caring about someone. When I closed out all of the static in my mind and just cared, truly cared about them! I know the other person felt it as well, because in a world where it is hard to find somebody that cares, when someone finally does it is beautiful, it's powerful. Truly caring about someone else is one of the ways you find the greatness and goodness in yourself. It is one of the ways you find your true self.

Food had become an issue again, in that I hadn't been out hunting in several days because of the rain and my meditation moments. We take for granted all that we have at our disposal. Even the poorest people have food to eat when they want to eat it. It is easy not to take things for granted when you don't have them. But like most things, we don't spend time appreciating them until they are gone. Living a life appreciating what you have is truly living life.

There was a big downed tree about forty yards down, and I tried searching for some grubs. As I dug and pushed the largest section over, I found a storehouse of the bugs. I had seen guys on TV eating grubs before, and they didn't seem to mind. The first one went down a little hard, but soon I realized that taste was something we had made up and that the body didn't really care. Food only has one purpose, and that is to sustain the body. My body was indifferent to the taste, not to mention this was all I had at the moment. I ate about ten or twenty and then put the rest in my pockets for later.

If my family could see me now, I thought. They would see me on my knees hungry and eating grubs, like an animal. What a sight I must have been. I had long hair, a beard, and was much thinner. My clothes looked worse than any homeless person, and I had scratches and cuts all over my body. Would I starve before the cancer got me? I never stopped thinking about the fact that this would become more about surviving the wilderness than about the cancer. More and more that reality was becoming the truth, but at the same time this natural diet without processing and preservatives seemed to have a positive effect and was hopefully slowing the growth of the beast inside me.

I was still hungry, and the rain continued to fall, which made it impossible to fish. I hadn't seen any game for days except for a few deer. It's not easy to kill a deer if you don't have a gun, but I was going to have to do something or I would starve. Looking back on my life, I couldn't remember a time when I went hungry. I might have missed a meal or two from being too busy or when I was in college and had to skip a meal from lack of money, but never was food not available to me.

After two days of eating grubs and berries, I decided to go hunting. I needed meat, something that would give me energy and strength. I needed something big, like a deer. I knew where the game trail was and left to go there. Climbing up in the tree that was right on the trail, I waited for an unsuspecting deer to come along. My thoughts were that I would jump from the tree and stab it with my knife. I was getting weaker, though, and I hoped I would have the strength and stamina to finish it.

Hours went by and nothing. My body was cramping, and I wondered if it would be able to move if the chance came. Then just as I was starting to give up, a small doe started coming up the trail. My pulse was racing, and I felt life come back to my weakened muscles. As I prepared to jump, something was taking over in me, some natural instinct. I had never felt so alive. All my senses were turned on and in a heightened state. I had always talked to Lisa about the fact that I never really felt alive and how much I wanted that. The closest I had ever come was when I was riding my mountain bike on some rugged terrain and stood the chance of getting hurt. Now, here I was, feeling more alive than ever, yet on the brink of death.

I could hear every noise. I felt my heart beating and the air coming in and out of my lungs. Then time just seemed to stop; everything went into slow motion. I leaped from the tree, falling exactly on the target. I plunged my knife deep into the side of the deer, and we struggled for what seemed like an hour. Though I was a little bigger, I was outmatched in strength and power. I held on with all my might and didn't let go. Branches were hitting me in my face, and I felt my legs smashing on the rocks as we plowed through the trees. Finally she lay over and took her last breath. It was an odd feeling. I didn't know whether to feel elated or sad for what I'd done, but the hunger pangs urged me on. Exhausted and emotional, I cut off the hindquarter first, thinking it would be the easiest to carry. I'd come back and get the rest later. Dragging the meat up the side of the canyon back to Lazarus, I felt like a caveman.

As I cooked up my life-giving meal, I thought about the fact that out of all the meals I'd eaten in my life, I'd never thought about where they had came from. I just took for granted that it was there.

Not this time. I appreciated every bite I took like never before. I wished I would have taken the time to appreciate more when I had the chance. But isn't that just how we are? We want and we want, but after we get it, we don't care about it anymore, and then the cycle starts all over again with something else.

After eating my fill, I went down to recover the rest of the meat. As I got closer, I heard a very strange grunting, and before I knew it I had scared a very large badger that was indulging in the rest of the meat. In an instant, he was on me. I turned and tried to run, but he was faster. When I finally tripped, he lunged at me and started slashing at me with his massive claws. His large teeth came within inches of tearing me apart. I was truly in a fight for my life, and it was terrifying. I did everything to keep him off. I kicked and screamed, threw rocks and dirt. He was trying to kill me.

Again I was fighting for my life, but not from the cancer. I grabbed a small log and just started hitting him as hard as I could. He was bloody and screaming loudly at me; I was bloody and screaming at him. I pounded away with all my might, aware that this could be the end for me if I failed. I finally caught him with a blow to the side of the head, and he let out a screech and angrily ran away. I won the battle this time, but I would never want to see him again. I might not be so lucky next time. With the energy I had left, I quickly scrambled away like a whipped pup, not waiting for him to come back for more. I still had some meat left over, but I would have to hunt again, next time not waiting so long to get the rest. He could have this one.

That night, I was reminded of how many kids we are rearing who could not take care of themselves if they had to. Not that I was doing such a great job of taking care of myself, but so many of the things I learned as a kid were helping me survive now. We have gotten to a point where the only thing we teach our kids is how to live in the illusion we have created. I didn't know any boys that could change a spark plug in a lawn mower. And I didn't know any that could feed themselves if they had to hunt and prepare their food, not to mention having to fight for it.

We don't really prepare our youth for what life is going to be like. We all say they will have to learn just like we did. It's like we are afraid to talk to them about the incredible possibilities of life, afraid that it might look like we failed at ours. It's hard to say to a kid you need to do this or that when you're not doing it yourself, so, out of embarrassment, we don't say anything. The perpetuation of the process just continues, and our kids grow up making the same mistakes we did.

If I was able to talk to a young person right now, I would show him the bad decisions I had made and the things I'm doing wrong even now, and show him the right way, a better way to increase the quality of his life, to live a more purposeful life, a richer, more powerful life based on truth. It's better to learn from someone that has been there and done that and can guide you based on experience.

Somehow I think it should be mandatory for young men to join the Boy Scouts or some sort of boys' club and learn other ways of taking care of themselves and others. I wished I had. Most fathers today are just too busy to teach their kids survival education, or they don't know themselves. In fact, how many kids ever even get to go camping? I know dads who have never taken their kids fishing. In the life we live today, somebody does everything for you. Somebody fixes your car, builds your deck, teaches your kids to play football, paints your walls, and mows your lawn. I'm not thinking it's wrong or right, but what will our kids end up like? They will be able to connect to the Internet and Google help.

Will they even wonder what feeling alive is like when all of their education comes from a box hooked up to the Internet? Will they have values? Will they know the satisfaction of building something with their hands? So many young men today look and act so feeble. Many are overweight and would lie down and cry if they were in a life-or-death situation. The scary thing is that these kids will become our future leaders and the fathers of our future children.

Like it or not, the fact is we are hardwired. There are things that were put in our minds from the beginning. A woman needs to look at her mate and feel secure and protected. She needs to feel strength and power in her man. I wondered if women in the future would even need a man. In our society, men are not learning how to be men, and emasculation is at an all-time high. Men have forgotten and suppressed the very essence of what makes them men. They don't get sweaty and dirty anymore; they don't get cuts and bruises. I knew friends who didn't even have a toolbox.

I know all this sounds silly, but some things will never change. Men and woman still have a role to play. Men still need to be men, and women still need to be women. I remembered when Lisa would be so excited when I would fix the window that wouldn't shut or unclog the dishwasher. She would even get excited when I would come in from working on the lawn mower. She said it was something to do with the grease on my hands and the smell. I hardly knew any of my friends that could or would attempt to change the oil in their car.

Doug's life had been like that. His father was a successful banker and his mother a schoolteacher. Doug grew up at the country club. Everything was done for him. I was the first person who took him fishing. He pranced around the pond like a little girl afraid of getting his boots muddy. I remembered a time I started wrestling with him. He couldn't fight his way out of a wet paper sack, and this was a man who weighed two hundred pounds. I almost felt ashamed of myself as I bullied him. Afterwards, he hung his head down and asked me how he got so pathetic. If Doug had it to do over, what would he do differently?

That night my mind felt so strong. Mentally, spiritually, I felt very powerful. I was focused. I felt like Superman but in a spiritual way. I had survived a battle with death from a monster, and so far I was surviving the cancer. As I lay there, I stared up into the heavens. *It is time for the rain to stop,* I thought. I envisioned the clouds separating and the rain moving on elsewhere. I believed that I could stop the rain. I believed I could make it rain. I believed I could make anything happen by just saying the words.

The next morning when I awoke, the sun was shining again and there was no rain. I couldn't help but smile and start to believe.

Week Eight:

MEETING THE NEIGHBORS/ I WANT TO LIVE

Sunday

I'm not writing as often as I did at first because I have so much that I am doing and experiencing that is too difficult to put into mere words. I hope whoever reads this journal will understand and know that this time, up here alone, is the most intimate spiritual experience of my entire life, and to try to put the thoughts and feelings into mortal words would be so insufficient.

The new experiences and revelations were coming faster and faster. I only hoped I could keep up. My outlook on my life and all of life was changing in ways I never could have imagined. Though the process of deep diving into my life continued, I started seeing things in a more positive light; I started seeing the light. I'm even starting to understand the words given to me.

It was time to get back out and start hunting again. As always, food was a dominating issue. The smell was just incredible, and everything seemed so alive. As I stared out, I could almost see the energy of the plants and trees. The life in everything seemed to be speaking to me. I felt sorry for all the people who had not experienced this extraordinary feeling. Even though I was dying, I had never felt so in tune with life. I thought again of the moment when I would pass from this life to the next. That was one of the most important reasons I was here. I wanted to know the exact moment that I left this world. I wanted to know the last thing I saw, the last thing I was thinking, as close to God as I could be, no veil between us. What would it be like? Would there be a great light like in the journey to the stars I had? Would I be able to hear, to feel? Would I still have a body? This had always been the greatest mystery to me, life after death.

If you subscribe to conventional religion, there is either heaven or hell, and there would be a whole process that would take place. Man, have I ever struggled with that whole thing. Could it be that the Bible teachings are right? And if you don't follow those rules, then you would end up in this fire pit somewhere underground with the devil forever. The whole notion of sin and the Ten Commandments has haunted me for years. What about all the other religions? Are they wrong? Are they right? Or is there a true doctrine that must be followed?

For the most part, my whole life I had prayed to God every day, asking for forgiveness for my sins, and then continued to sin, based on the teachings of the Bible. I would pray for answers and guidance and then not listen. I would walk with one foot in and one foot out, never really committed to a religious doctrine. Somewhere in my mind that always caused some confusion. I really knew what

I wanted but didn't have the resilience to make it happen on a daily basis. It was like I decided and knew what to do and how to do it but just never could make that stance.

I've asked God all the above questions, as I'm sure a lot of people have. Maybe others don't ask directly, but in their minds I'm certain they have wondered the same things. I have felt that God has guided, protected, and helped me my whole life. I'm not sure what my life would have been like if it were not for my belief and faith in God and His presence in my life. Though I have questioned and at times abandoned my faith, something in me keeps me coming back. Each time I come back the voice gets louder in my head. Each time I get down on my knees I stand up taller. And every time I ask questions, more is revealed than I asked. In my heart I just really wanted to totally surrender to God, to devote myself to him and his purpose for my life.

My friends and family never knew what this meant to me. Not that I hid my beliefs, but the topic just never came up. And if it did, I stayed clear of the subject of religion because more times than not it was just one of them trying to prove their way of thinking was right. My view was always what works for you is the right way, and I'd never judged anyone for their own spiritual beliefs.

So what do I believe? I believe there is a supreme creator I call God. I believe He put all of us here and that He does speak to us or put into our minds and hearts the awareness and wisdom of His presence. I believe that we are here for a reason and that there is much more to this existence than we are aware of. I've read many books on religion and self-help books and believe there is some truth in all of them, just like the Bible. I also think that the evolutionists are right in some of their theories. I just don't believe that any one of them is the only way and that we are too limited as humans to understand the entire dynamics of it all. Maybe in the days to come a different truth will be revealed.

The way I've lived my life is much the same way I've believed in religion. I feel that love is the most important emotion there is.

I believe that with love comes power—power over disease, financial conditions, happiness, emotional well-being, and all other factors in life. One of my favorite things to say is that "I'm in love with life and life is in love with me." I have tried to live a life of truth. I try not to lie to myself or others. I've tried to not hurt others. I've tried to be a good man. I have failed plenty along the way, and I have been successful along the way. But as I have found out on this journey, there is a whole other level of being, a whole other way to love, and to get there takes commitment, discipline, self-analysis, and a desire to live a joyous life. I don't try to convince others to think or believe the way I do. I may challenge them to expand their thoughts or to consider something different, but I know that each person has his own truth and the responsibilities that come with it. The responsibilities that come with the way you believe and act are the real truth.

Life is a decision-making process of creating what is to be your life. It's about making the decisions that make your life what it is or what it is not. This series of decisions that you make and learn from are the ultimate truths about your life. So my own decision to believe in God and then to make decisions based on that has created who I am today. I made the choice to live out my last days at Lazarus Ledge instead of a hospital bed on morphine and hooked up to machines. I wanted and needed to get as close to God as I could prior to passing from this life to the next. I needed to cleanse my mind and body; I needed to truly understand the life that I had lived.

Monday

I set out for the day with a sense of urgency to find food. I knew I was going to have to travel farther out than I had previously. The reality of dying of something other than cancer was a driving force. Up until then I had been lucky not to fall off of some cliff, starve, or get killed by an animal. There are so many things that can happen to you in the mountains. Every step could be your last. A broken leg or bad cut could be lethal. Getting lost and losing your mind is always a possibility.

I continued on with my sights on the next canyon over, hoping to find something to eat. I bet that I'd lost at least fifteen pounds, some of which I probably didn't need, but I was very thin. As before, my instincts and senses were kicking in. I truly felt alive and on point.

Crossing over the first mountain that would lead me into the canyon, I caught out of the corner of my eye a very large snake sunning itself on top of a rock. That snake only represented one thing to me: a meal. Like a predator, I started stalking. Slowly I moved with purpose, and as I got closer, I saw it was a large rattlesnake. He looked to be about four feet long and mean as the devil. One bite from this guy and my life was finished. I'd never been afraid of snakes—spiders, yes—but still I was very nervous and cautious. I had to make a decision to either surprise rush attack him or slowly, deliberately attack. The rush attack came over me before I even had time to think about it, and within seconds, I had taken my walking stick and pounded his head off. As I sat there still panting, waiting for the abatement of the adrenaline rush, I decided to cut the long fangs out and keep the rattler for some of the things I had been making. The skin would work for decoration as well.

I had eaten rattlesnake before in restaurants and always thought it was good. Now I wasn't eating for a delicacy but for my own survival. I had started to peel back the skin when a noise over to the right startled me. All at once a large black bear was charging me. Bears look big on TV, but in real life they look like monsters. Although this bear was a common black bear and stood no more than four feet high, at the moment of his attack, he appeared at least twenty feet high. My studies had told me black bears are indigenous only to the U.S. and can be found anywhere from Florida to the frozen tundra areas of the north. Brown bears are found only in Alaska and are much bigger than the black bears.

The fear that struck me was a fear like I had never known before. I started running, falling down along the way. I just knew by the look in that bear's eyes that if I didn't escape I would become his next meal. I had read and heard many times that in case of a bear attack you shouldn't run. That did not appear to be the logical choice at this time. I just ran. I ran faster than I had ever dreamed. He charged at me with the speed of a bullet. In an instant, I was on the ground.

When I looked up, all I saw was teeth and claws. Black bears have huge claws, good for climbing trees and also good for taking the skin of a skinny man with one big swipe. Remembering my knife, I pulled it out and started slashing, stabbing. It felt like I was using a sewing needle to let the air out of a tire.

He stopped his assault for a moment, as if irritated, and when he did, I got up and started running again. I don't know how far I ran, but when I finally decided to look back, it became apparent that all he really wanted was my dinner and not me. I let him have the snake since I felt further confrontation with the bear might be to my disadvantage. On my way out of there, I had to smile to myself. I had fought a bear over food, and even though the bear had won, I came out of it alive. Yes!

I should have felt small in comparison to the abilities of the other creatures around me, but I couldn't. I was competing on their level even though they had been born with the innate knowledge of hunting in this environment while I came from a city with a McDonald's or Starbucks on every corner. I was elated. I was on equal footing with a bear. How awesome was that? At some point I would have to learn to fight my way through these situations, stand up to them, but for now I was glad to be accepted as equal. For now I would have to get down to the valley and hope to catch a fish or find some berries to eat.

After the adrenaline left my system, I was out of energy. I made my way down to the stream. As I sat there on a rock, I threw up. I didn't know if it was from the fear or just hunger, but what scared me was what I saw in the liquid. It was blood, and it had a very foul smell. My insides hurt badly, and my head was pounding. I had deep wounds from the bear's claws and cuts from falling down. It was an overall horrible, excruciating feeling. My previous euphoria was once again replaced with illness and fear.

I made a small fire and lay there in pain and fear wondering what was going on. I dozed off, and when I awoke, I was even weaker and still hungry. I prayed.

God, I need Your help. I'm scared, hungry, and sick. Please show me the way. Provide for me like You always have. Give me strength; give me power over this. Help me see and understand what You are tying to teach me, please.

As I sat there in pain and scared out of my mind, all I could think of was the safety of my home. I was tired, weak, and hungry. This was the first time since I had been here that I really felt defeated. I felt pitiful, alone. I wished I could just take my last breath and be done with this. I'm not where I needed to be yet, and I don't want to leave this life here in this condition, but I'm just worn out.

Rocking back and forth in so much pain, I started thinking about the whole process. I've come so far, digging so deep into myself. Getting so close to God, getting so close to the truth about me and who I am, what we are. Which was it going to be? My inability to overcome the elements or the cancer that will take my life?

I thought about my family. How much I loved them, how much I would miss them. How would all of this change their lives? Would they learn anything from this, or would they be embarrassed at what I had done? This must seem so selfish of me. How could anyone understand what I've done? What would they say at my funeral? Would they have a funeral for me? If I pass from this life to the next out here, alone, who will know? My body will be consumed by vultures, and all that will be left of me is what is on Lazarus Ledge and this journal, and it may never be found.

Once again I looked back on my life from childhood to this point. *All those years that my mind, my life, and my emotions were consumed with such trivial matters were a waste,* I thought. I allowed insignificant things to take up most of my waking hours. I let fear and worry and anxiety dictate my daily life. If I just had it to do again, there was so much I would change. I would have moved with such purpose. I would have let go of all of the trash in my mind. I would have spent more time with me. I would have forgiven quickly, loved faster. Why do we have to get to a point in our lives like the one I was in right now before we see the truth? This is truly an incredible experience we have here, this thing called life. There are so many wonderful possibilities, so much happiness to be had. If I could just look into someone's eyes right now and touch them. If I could just spend some time with my family right now, there are so many things I could tell them.

As I continued to review my life and the things I thought about the most, it amounted to this: money, sex, work, things I wanted, pain from arguments, things other people wanted from me, guilt, insecurities, doubt, anger, the past. How could I have let all these things dominate thoughts on a daily basis? What purpose did any of these serve? Were any of these things eternally significant? What would I have done with my life if I had known what I know now? What could I have done with my life? I know that if you are living with stress, anxiety, pain, guilt, and fear, you're not living; you are dying a slow, painful death.

I thought about all the drama, issues, and struggles I had experienced, and for what? What made me do the things I did? What makes us? As I sat there thinking of all these things, I found myself screaming out, "Does anybody hear me? Does anybody hear me? Stop now, stop now; choose differently; make better decisions; live to love, and love to live; let go of yesterday; live now; be happy; be healthy; live with peace! An amazing life is yours to be lived!"

With all that on the table, I sat there cold and weak. I was faced with a question that I'd thought about many times. *Am I really who I say I am?* I always, for the most part, felt that I was. Do we live a lie when it comes to who we present ourselves to be? It seems that we carry around all these little lies about ourselves, trying to convince ourselves and the people around us who we are, always afraid that someone will find us out. So we continually make up new lies every day to cover up the existing ones. This process never seems to end. Then we get to a point that we really don't know who we are because we have repeated the lies so many times. We look in the mirror every day and see nothing. Here we are, looking at ourselves, but we don't see anything, just a face, a body, and a façade. Then we spend the rest of the time trying to figure out what other people think we are. We don't know ourselves, so we don't know what we are to anybody else.

We wear certain clothes, drive certain cars. We live in homes we think make a statement about who we are. All the things we do and use to try to convince other people of who we are are all part of the lie we live. We spend all this time trying to convince all the people around us that what they see is who we are, but is it really?

I went into a deep meditation and started cleaning out my mind, soul, and spirit of all my own little lies, all of the things that I'd made up about myself. There where so many lies, a lifetime's worth. I heard all the things that people told me I was—my mother, my father, and my friends. No wonder I was so confused; no wonder we are all so confused. So many people influence our thoughts and opinions on who we are supposed to be. We listen to all that and then add our own distorted truth, and the result is complete and utter confusion.

I dug deep. I wanted everything out. Every opinion, every state-ment from others, and everything I had created. I needed, wanted, to be left with nothing, no false perceptions. I wanted to be left with only the truth of this moment, much like the animals around me. This took some time, but in the end, I felt like me, just me, and it brought a great feeling of peace and power. To christen this new feeling, I walked down to the lake. I would wash away any leftover residue. I would cleanse myself of all the emotions and this pain that was consuming me.

The lake was breathtakingly beautiful, deep, and surrounded by large rocks and trees. I felt like I was the first one who had ever seen it. The water itself was crystal clear and calm. It looked magical and as if it had healing powers. As I took off my clothes and prepared to jump in, I felt how naked I really was. Just like I had planned, here I stood naked in life, just like the day I was born. My mind was clear, and my soul was alive. I felt transparent to the world.

I took a deep breath and thanked God for this moment, and I realized how in the moment I really was. I was not hearing all the voices, all the static. I looked up and then back down to the depths below. With a big, deep breath, I jumped as far out as I could. It felt like it was minutes before I actually hit the water. Quickly and all at once, I was brought back to a harsh reality when my body sensed the temperature of the water. It was ice cold. The shock of the water locked up every muscle in my body, and fear and panic screamed throughout my head. I was only about twenty feet from where I leaped in, but at that moment it looked like a mile. Gasping and splashing about, I struggled to make it back to the rocks, only to find that all the boulders and rocks were covered with a slimy coat of moss. I could not get a hold. I looked to the right and the left, but the shoreline was the same. Fifteen feet up from where I had jumped was safety.

I tried to pull myself up on a rock to rest but kept sliding off. Freezing cold, weak, and tired, I continued trying to climb up, grasping, reaching. My muscles were cramping, and the thought came into my mind once again. It was not the cancer that was going to kill me but the place I had chosen to come to God.

I was not ready to die here. I longed for the warmth of the fire and the security of my home. At that moment, something came over me, a strong emotion that I can only describe as an out-of-body experience. It was like I was looking down upon myself from above. I could see myself splashing about, trying to reach up for a hold on a rock. I saw myself going under, sinking. I saw myself drowning. As I was sucked back into my body, I started screaming at the top of my lungs, "I want to live! I don't want to die! God I want to live!"

At once I turned around and started swimming across the lake. There, about three hundred yards away on the other side, was a flat bank where I could climb out of the freezing water. I had no strength left, and the chances of making it across were slim. I had no energy left, and I couldn't feel my body; it was numb from the cold. It might as well have been ten miles to the other side, but I had no other options.

As I started to swim across the lake, I started thinking about how precious life really is. One moment you are standing on a rock totally in the moment and filled with life, and the next you are looking at the end of your life. What a perfect design; how beautiful it all is. All of the devastating moments that we are faced with in our lives, when we think we just can't go on, that we can't live another moment and we have reached our end, are just new benchmarks. They are moments to help us see life in a different way. They make us recreate ourselves. They make us expand our realities. No one wants to experience these things, but without them, we simply would never grow.

It dawned on me how much I really love life. There I was struggling to swim to save my life, not knowing if I would make it or not but thinking how perfect it all was. I found myself looking around at the mountains and canyons as I kicked, thrashed, and gasped inch by inch across the lake, totally appreciating my situation. If I made it out of this, there would not be another moment I would fear this cancer or anything else. I would appreciate every moment, for every moment is an opportunity to change your life. I would look at it as a chance I might never have had to become the real me, to understand what I can truly be.

When I looked up, I was there just feet from the bank. I'm not sure how long it took or how I did it, but I lay there with mud in my hands. I crawled up onto the bank, naked and cold. Tears poured out. This moment had made the rest of all the little things in my life that had looked so threatening look silly in comparison. Even the hunger I felt seemed to be insignificant. Live every moment like it was your last. So true!

I had a long walk back and would have to leave my clothes and bag behind. There was no way to get back to where I had jumped in. So, naked and tired, I started back. There stood in my way large canyons and rough terrain. But all I could think of was some food and a warm fire. That was true motivation like I had never before experienced. With hours of rough hiking in front of me, tired and cold and naked as the fish in the water, I started thinking about the world and the things that happen every day that shouldn't. Why do people do the things they do? It seemed so clear that it's just not okay. There should not be child molestation, cruelty, and homelessness. There shouldn't be starvation and pollution. There shouldn't be suicide and depression. I thought for hours of all these things. What could I, what could we, ever do about all of it? I did not know. Was God challenging me?

As I clawed my way through the trees and canyons, feeling every branch and sharp object jab into my cold, sensitive skin, I felt a certain hope come over me in regards to the way we could change the world. At first, it seemed to me that I was hallucinating; how naïve to think that all of the troubles of this world could be changed, but in my situation, all things were a lot clearer. What could I do? I was in the mountains dying of cancer or dying of one thing or another every day.

I laid down on some pine needles and covered up to get warm, still sick and hurting. I fell into a deep sleep. That now-common dream with a haze came over me. Like before, I couldn't tell if it was a dream or a vision. I was there in the dream, but at the same time I was not.

The dream started with the vision of a block meeting in a small city. Everyone on the block was there. They were discussing the same things that I had thought of earlier, the things that shouldn't happen in the world. They were discussing each other's issues and challenges. They were open and caring, truly feeling for one another. From there, the block meeting turned into a town and then city meeting. Again all the people in the area, from the homeless to the criminals, from the young and single to the established elderly, were there still discussing their problems and issues and coming together, helping each other, supporting each other.

The city meeting turned into a county meeting and then a state meeting, all the while bringing everyone in the area together. Murderers, thieves, people thinking of suicide, they were all there. I saw people holding each other, crying. They were seeing the possibilities of hearts, souls, and minds coming together with a purpose.

The meeting was duplicated simultaneously all over the world, and there was no fighting. People started letting go of all the reasons they felt gave them the right to do the things they had been doing. They started looking at life differently. Instead of hate, they felt love; instead of fear, they felt hope; instead of resentment, they felt forgiveness, and there was a great peace that came upon the people. And one day after another the world continued to change.

When I awoke, I lay there for a while and thought about what I had just dreamed. It seemed ridiculous, but given the things that happen in our world every day, anything is possible. What a great way to bring people together to discuss the truth.

Sometime later I managed to make it back to Lazarus Ledge. I was never so happy to see my meager refuge. I got some clothes on, built a fire, warmed up some of the meat I had saved, and made some tea from pine needles. My feet and hands were cut and bloody, and I looked like I had been in a fight with a rosebush. I tended to the cuts so they wouldn't get infected. The warmth of the fire and the food in my belly restored me, and I began to feel like I didn't have a care in the world. I was happy to be alive, even in this state. That night I sat by my warming fire and continued working on the ornaments I was making.

I had survived a lot up to this point. At no other time in my life had I ever been this challenged, this defeated, and come back to thank God for the experiences. At no time had I ever appreciated my life more. At no time had I ever been so alive.

The little fire and the warm clothes on my back were the greatest gifts I had ever received. I began thinking of things that had once made me happy and giddy with excitement, like my first new car, my Rolex watch. Things like that seemed empty and meaningless now. How happy I would feel now just to have a new pair of shoes, any shoes.

Tuesday

During the night I thought about all the people in
the world who were dying—some of diseases, some in car accidents, and some from the hand of another human being. Where are they in their lives? Did they have a chance to even think about it? Did they even care? What about all the people who were depressed, addicted to drugs and alcohol, and the many who are struggling with relationships? How could I let them know what I had discovered? How could I get them to look at life differently? How could I convince others to make different choices, better choices? How could I help them understand how beautiful life is, what the possibilities are?

We are not cursed. We are not victims. We are not doomed to struggle and fail. We can be everything we choose to be. Life can and will be exactly what we choose it to be. It will be incredible to the extent that we can imagine. God gave us power over our thoughts, power over our emotions, and power over our lives. I choose to be an angel, an angel with a message. I feel the beginnings of a purpose.

I lay there watching the fire and started thinking of all the situations that people were going through at that very moment. I reached out to them. I could see thousands of different things taking place. I could hear all the voices. I could feel all the emotions. One by one, I viewed them. I became a part of their experience. I listened to them pour their hearts out and reach out for help. It's not that I had any magic answers, any surefire way of curing any problems, but from where I sat, there was nothing but love and truth in my heart and mind. I talked to each of them about what I had learned on my journey. There were many who still could not look outside of their situation, but there were more who listened and made decisions based on what I shared with them.

There was one man in particular who was so distraught that he saw no alternative but to end his life. He had created a life of struggles, hurt, and confusion. He had been recently divorced, he was broke, and he was unhealthy. He was consumed with guilt, pain, and resentment. He felt there was no future left for him. The pain he was in was overwhelming not just for him but for me as well. What do you tell someone who finds it a challenge to take another breath, someone who sees no hope in the next day? There were so many years of guilt and hurt and pain in him. He no longer believed in himself or life. There are so many people in the same situation to varying degrees. You may see them in the grocery store or at work and just don't know what they are going through. It may be financial woes. It may have to do with a relationship. Or it could be a combination of a hundred other things. Everyone is fighting a battle.

The only thing I could tell him was to start over. I mean really start over. Tomorrow would be the first day of the rest of his life. Why not? As kids, we did it all the time. When the game you were playing did not work in your favor, you yelled out, "Do over!" and in most cases you did. There is always a "do-over" in life as long as you are still alive. You don't have to get permission from anybody or fill out any papers. This is a simple truth that we don't take advantage of often enough. If you no longer want to be who or what you are, just start over. It doesn't matter what it is. If you no longer want to be depressed, if you no longer want to be addicted to things, if you want to have a great relationship, if you want to be healthy, start over. Begin by having a clear idea of who you want to be and what you want to be, and start over. Let go of what was. The key to starting over is to not start *all* over. You hear people say that all the time, "I guess I will wake up tomorrow and start all over again." The *all* in that sentence means you are bringing the *all* with you and doing it *all* over again. When you start over, you want to start over fresh and new, not bringing the *all* from yesterday with you. We do have the ability to take advantage of this loophole, and it can change your life. "Start over," wake up in the morning, and create what you want. Leave the *all* behind where it belongs.

So with this man that was exactly what we did. But before making changes, we took an inventory of all the things that got him to the point of desolation so he wouldn't make some of the same decisions as before. Then we decided what the new life would look like. How he wanted to feel, what he wanted to look like, where he wanted to live, how he wanted to think, how he wanted to treat and be treated by others. So one by one he let go of each thought about his current situation, getting rid of all the trash in his mind, all the limiting thoughts, and preparing for the next day that would be the start of the new life he was creating. A new life based on truth, forgiveness, passion, love. A new life that allowed him to be what God intended him to be.

When the vision ended I didn't know whether to be happy or sad. Even though I felt like one man's life had been changed, there were so many more that needed help, crying out for answers and healing. I didn't even know if these visions were real or not. Was this God showing me my future, my purpose?

Could it really be that simple? Can we just start over? I know that in my life if someone had told me that, I would have told them they were naïve or just didn't understand my situation. But if we can make life that complicated, why can't we also make it that simple? Yes, we can start over, every minute, every hour, every day, day after day. For the rest of our lives, each time getting better and improving. Each start over you clean up the mistakes, stop the patterns, and create the way you want to feel and act. It makes no difference what you did or what happened to you yesterday. You can move on and start over. I think sometimes you have to look beyond everything you have been taught and believe to be able to see your existence in a completely different way. Let go of yourself! *Carpe diem!* Grab today and seize the moment! Decide who and what you will be today.

I decided to make my day as simple as I could. I would do my best not to think of anything. I would just lay on the ground and let the energy from the earth move through me. I stared at a flower until I had enjoyed every part of it. I focused on the air I was breathing until I could feel it coursing through my lungs. I listened to the sound of the creek becoming part of the water itself. I studied a rock until I could see into its core. I practiced starting over with my thoughts minute by minute. I shut my eyes and took a journey through my body. That was my day. Why had I never done this before? Everyone should make a day like this. There is no reason that we can't. There is no reason why we shouldn't.

Forty-three years I had been alive, and for forty-three years, I used each day to complicate my life further, to make it harder than it had to be. Why would I choose that over a life of simplicity, a life of truth, a life of happiness and joy? I wrote this to remind me:

As the wind blows across my damp face, I feel things.

The sun shines in my eyes, and I understand.

My bare feet upon the grass bring me clarity.

The life all around me inspires me.

The death makes me urgent.

My eyes open, and I start all over again

As if on a journey to a distant star,

Knowing not how far or how near,

Just a journey.

Having been here before,

I know it will take more than one leg to complete,

But one in front of the other brings me closer,

If only the length of a thought,

Said he.

Week Ten:

THEY WEREN'T WRONG

Monday

I just focused on God, just feeling His presence in my life and all that He had created. Over the years, I have spent many hours contemplating the whole concept of God. Who is God's God? How could there have been just God? He had to come from some-where. How did He create all of this? Are there other civilizations out there? The questions have been many.

What one question would change your entire life, if you knew the answer? If you knew the answer to that question, what would your life be like tomorrow? How would you feel? What would you do? How would your life change? Would you worry about the things you concern yourself with today? Would you care about that new car you wanted? Would you love differently? And what is that question that for most of us would change our lives forever? Is there really a God? Does He really exist? Does He really know who I am, and does He hear me?

All my life I have pondered these questions, as I know many others have as well. I have thought about how my life would change if God appeared and sat down beside me and made Himself known to me. What would I do next? How would I proceed with my life? What questions would I ask?

Some years ago before Lisa, I was really struggling with life and trying to figure it all out. I was stressed out and anxiety ridden, drinking too much, and there was nothing but drama in my life, all self-created of course. Life was consuming me from every angle, and I was depressed. I was experimenting with drugs, and I had some friends in my life that were not healthy for me. It's not that I had it bad. Quite the opposite, I seemingly had everything you could want—money, great job, toys—but my life was empty. There was nothing that made sense to me. I questioned everything, why there was so much drama, so many struggles, and so much pain. I questioned why people lied, cheated, deceived. There was just so much crap all the time. You just don't see at the time what all that does to your life. Over time it can be one of the most potent poisons there is.

In the end, I let go of the only thing in my life that I trusted: my belief in my Creator, my belief in God. Things didn't get better; in fact, the confusion got worse. At night, I would lie awake in bed and literally fight demons from pulling at my legs, trying to pull me down even further. All night, they would come at me, grabbing, pulling, and watching for me to give in. I would get up in the morning soaked with sweat and worn out and start all over, bringing with me the issues from the day before.

One evening after a night of drinking, drugs, and carousing, I came home and looked around with disgust at what my life had become. I had just had it with everything. I was unhealthy, emotionally distraught, and sick of life. I really didn't want to go on and considered my options.

As I stood there with my option in my hand, something happened. Something came over me that I had never felt. It was a feeling that came from deep within. Instantly, I was dropped to my knees. I didn't choose to go down to my knees. I was literally dropped to my knees. With my head between my legs, I started bawling. I was in extreme pain, unimaginable pain, but had little control over what I was doing. For hours I sat there on the floor wondering what was next. Slowly, as the tears subsided and my eyes opened again, something started happening. God started talking to me, showing me where my life was headed, and it wasn't pretty, even worse than it was. He showed me the other way it could be and told me I had a choice. That all I had to do was choose it.

Now does that prove that there is a God? No, but from that day forward, I can say that something worked through me in my life like never before, and now when I ask the question, things come into my view that are proof enough for me. Even as I sit thinking of all this, I feel the oxygen coming into my lungs and the blood coursing through my veins. I think about emotions and feelings that I have. I think about how my eyes work. On and on thoughts come to my mind, and I no longer try to prove there is not a God.

I am.

I am beautiful because I am a reflection of my Creator.

I breathe because my Father said to.

I am pure because I am born of purity.

I have vision so I can see what was created for me.

I love because my Father gave me the opportunity to experience a part of Him.

I create because my Father is creation.

I heal because my Father is a healer.

I forgive because my Father is a forgiver.

I live because my Father gives life.

For I am my Father's son and I am a son of my Father.

I still struggle living by the teachings of the Bible and how they relate to my life. All this time that I felt I was right with God, that I was doing the right thing. Am I, in fact, right with God, really, or do I just make my religion fit my life like everything thing else? We have become pretty good at manipulating the truth and creating situations to fit our needs and lifestyle. I still and always have had this burning question in my mind. What if in the end I was wrong and I found myself without God? What if, because I didn't follow the teachings of Jesus and God by the letter, I was really not going to the next life and this was the end? What if?

As I took off in hunt of food, I started thinking about some of the stupid things I used to worry about. Was I smart enough? I would worry about how I looked. I would worry about how I sounded in conversations. I worried half my life away with stuff that nobody even cared about. If half of that time and energy were spent doing something about what I was worrying about, I wouldn't have had anything to worry about. Then I heard this:

Why do you worry so? Be still and know that I am God.

Seek only the path to me and your life will be light and free.

These words humbled me. What do you say to that statement? All I could think of was,

Never did I know I could feel so much.

Never did I know I could love so much.

Never did I know I had a soul.

Never did I know me,

And never did I know God.

All that I have been through is a small price to pay to know these things.

155

I hear you, my Father, and I know you are here. I won't question your presence again!

Tuesday

I got busy setting snares around, hoping for a varmint of any kind to fall into my trap. I would literally eat anything at this point. Now I know why every time I watched a nature show on TV, the animals were always doing the same thing: hunting for food. Every day now I understand and respect all the things that could take my life here. I know there is a real danger that I will die not from cancer but from something else. I know at some time I may not have enough energy to hunt, gather food, or defend myself.

As I looked at the traps I was building, I thought how archaic they were. But as I thought of all the cities in this world full of pollution from cars and manufacturing and trash, it dawned on me how antiquated we are as a society. It's hard for me to understand how we still use gasoline for our cars. It's hard for me to believe that we still pollute our environment to the point that soon everything that remains will be toxic. Why do we continue hunt animals to extinction? It's hard for me to believe we still have wars, that we still kill each other over land and religious beliefs. Why do we let these things continue? With the exception of technology, we really have not evolved at all. This is just not right; it is not okay!

I started to head toward the creek where I had caught trout before, hoping to at least get something in my stomach. Along the way, I kicked over fallen tree trunks and snatched up any bug I could catch. At this point, there was not much difference between me and the other animals of the forest. We were all just trying to survive. It would all be over soon enough. I thought back to my experience at the lake when I was faced with immediate death and the badger and the bear and how all I could think about then was living. I had to try to keep my head and not give up and remember those moments that I fought with all I had to live. I was not ready to die just yet.

Sitting down by the creek, I lay back and let my mind go.

Can we really create things in our lives with our thoughts? Is there really creative power in them? Do all the people who write all those books about changing your life by using the power of your mind know something the rest of us don't? I had seen and experienced some incredible things since I'd been here. As I thought about it, I realized that what they talk about in those books is not some mystical thing that happens out of thin air. It's not that we possess the power to perform magical things; it's even simpler than that. When you focus on something, you give your mind a roadmap, a source of action. Dreaming of winning the lottery will not win you the lottery, but it will give you a reason to get up and go buy a lottery ticket. Dreaming and thinking of starting your own business will not build the building for you, but it does inspire you to get out a sheet of paper and start putting a plan together. That is the power of your thoughts and the power you have to create what you want. To create great joy, great health, and great peace. I decided to try creating some food. How would the power of my thoughts create sustenance for my body? I pictured in my mind cooking a piece of meat over the fire and then sitting back and tasting the food as it went into my mouth. I did this over and over until it was as if I was really eating. I opened my eyes and became very alert and aware. I focused on my sense of hearing and my eyes, my smell. I recognized a scent I'd smelled before. I focused on the air around me carrying this smell, and after a while it was like I could see the molecules in the air. I got up and followed the scent, and fifty or sixty yards downstream I found the source. It was a deer that had gotten a leg stuck in between two rocks. It was fresh, and in just a few moments I had it cut up. I took some vines and tied all the meat together. I threw it over my back and started the trek back home. So I learned that we can also use our thoughts to turn our feelings and our hearts. We can use thoughts to turn on our senses and awareness. Shut your eyes, turn off the static, and go there.

About a half a mile back up the canyon, I felt a really bad pain in my midsection. It was like the pain that had made me go to the doctor in the first place. It was deep inside and shook my whole body. Down on my knees, face in the dirt, I grabbed the area that was causing all the pain. Dizziness came over me and then a torrent of more pain. I gasped for air and clawed at the excruciating pain. Without notice, a flood of liquid came pouring out of my body from everywhere it could. I couldn't control it, and within minutes I was laying in a puddle of muck that glistened red. It was obvious that a lot of it was blood, and like before at the lake, a fear came over me like no fear I had ever known. Was this it? Was it time?

With the loss of blood and certain dehydration, I became very weak and frail. I was hurting really bad, even worse than before. It felt like somebody was ripping out my insides. I was scared and filled with fear and still had a long way to go to get back to my camp.

I hadn't cried about the cancer yet, but now I was. The sight of the blood and the pain was horrifying. Laying there in the fetal position, all the thoughts I'd had about not having cancer were gone. Here the moment was that I had questioned just a few weeks ago. It was not just the cancer but also the elements working in unison to end my life. I felt like I was going to pass out at any moment. My head was reeling, and my body was screaming out. I had to get back to the camp. I had to settle up in my mind.

It took everything I had, crawling my way up the canyon wall inch by inch. I continued to vomit along the way. There were times I almost blacked out from the pain. Sweat soaked my clothes as I started burning up from fever. I reached inside my mind and pulled all the strength I had together. *God, give me just one more day. Give me a chance to pass on to You with a clear mind, not like this.*

Hours later I arrived at the entrance of the ledge. The name started to mean more to me than ever. Because I was truly on the ledge of life, or at least it felt like it. Unaware I had somehow managed to carry the meat of the deer in spite of being so sick and weak, I threw the dirt-covered meat down and built a fire. I drank some water and fell into what felt like a coma.

I woke up some hours later still feeling sick, a really bad sick, the worst sick I could imagine. I was a mess, dirty and grimy, liquid soaked. I cleaned myself up as best I could manage and got the fire going again. With my head between my legs, still clutching my stomach, I cried. I had been through so much since I had been here. There was no romance in this; all those thoughts had been left behind at the lake, with the bear, the badger, and now this sickening reality. What I thought I was doing here was fading fast. I was now left with a grim reality of a nasty, painful, agonizing death. I expected the pain would even get worse. Even the morphine in the end couldn't stop Doug's pain. He would literally beg for more. Now here I sat without even a Tylenol. How would I endure the pain?

I would have to learn how to deal with a lot in the days to come. I would find parts of my mind I never knew existed. I would have to find my power and use my mind to overcome the issues with my body. I would have to go to God many times.

I did my best to get some of the deer meat inside me, but every bite made me even sicker. The pine needle tea was about the only thing I could keep down. I was so tired that even the simplest task seemed overwhelming.

The pain was increasing hour by hour, and I struggled just to breathe. My goal all along was to be as close to God as I could before I passed, to truly have no veil between us, to know the exact moment that I left my body. Now, with all this pain, I couldn't even think about it. I just wanted to be medicated so I didn't feel anything. I knew I was not even close to what Doug must have felt, and I was already thinking of giving up. If I was to accomplish what I was here to do, I was going to have to become more powerful than I had ever been.

Friday

For a couple of days, all I did was sleep. In between the pain and trying to get food in me, I would weep. Sometimes while I was awake I would continue to work on the rings and bracelets just to take my mind off the situation. I also repaired my clothes, as they were getting pretty ragged. This helped me keep my mind off the pain a little. I tried to focus on anything else other than the pain. The bleeding continued, and some of the vomit was a scary color and smelled really bad. This truly was a terrible way to die!

In this world we live in, rarely do we ever see the real effects of someone dying. We all want to know the details, but most of us are not willing to say so. Most of the time we are far removed from the sometimes gruesome reality. Most of us are lured by thoughts of life ending, but rarely do we want to share the experience. We all struggle psychologically with the thought of our own death, that permanent unconsciousness where there may be nothing more than a void of life. That is probably why we seldom see people die.

Most death is hidden in a sterile, mystical place called hospitals. Doctors are great at masking the reality of what really happens, and it seems that it is over and done with before you know it. Our faces are hidden from death's face, and our ears aren't allowed to hear the icy shrills of the last moment. Though sometimes we are allowed a peek, it's just enough to flirt with the fascination that we really want to know what happens. Then it's all put into a pretty package and delivered.

Even with all of that happening to me, which includes all kinds of disgusting degradations, to be present with this biological, organic accumulation of the truth is horrifying but at the same time reassuring that I am alive. It's not the dignified death that I always thought would happen; there are no illusions of that, but every life that has been lived has been different, and I would imagine that every death will be as well.

I meditated a lot, trying to give myself power over the pain and fear. I would spend long hours breathing and focusing on the areas that hurt. The pain was intense. It must have been like being in labor twenty-four hours a day, never ending. As the pain got worse, I found it even more difficult to sleep, but there was also a sense of clarity that came with the pain, a sense of the struggle of life. There was no hiding from the reality of what I was experiencing. There was no magic pill, no denial to complicate matters. I thought about life and how we all spend a lifetime trying to avoid one form of pain or another. All of our pains and hurts are there for a reason. They help us reset our benchmarks. How great can we be if we don't know how evil we can be? How happy can we be if we don't know how sad we can be? Without knowing how bad we can feel, we can't know how good we can feel.

When I thought back to how many moments I didn't think I could continue on during this journey, I was reminded that even when things look bleak you are still doing more than you know. Even in those challenging moments I was chasing down rabbits and fighting bears. If I known just how bad it was going to be, I would have felt like a champion then. Don't forget to be happy when happiness is there. Don't forget to feel good when you feel good. Don't forget to feel loved when you are being loved. Take pleasure in it.

Sunday

After what must have been five days or so, I started moving around a little bit. Some of the pain had subsided at least enough that I could stand up, and I knew I had to get some sustenance in me. I'm not really sure what day it is, and frankly I don't really care. Each moment and day is just that.

I checked my traps and discovered a few successes. Berries and pine bark tea were still the best thing. Meat just didn't go down very well. Some days I even ate dirt because my body, for some unknown reason, was craving it. I burned a lot of sage because the smell helped my nausea and seemed to have a calming effect.

As bad as this all was, I was still grateful I was here and not hooked up to a bunch of machines with tubes sticking out of me, drugged up to the point I didn't even know who I was. Here, I truly knew who I was. I had cleared my mind, heart, and soul. There was no guilt, confusion, doubt, and no living in the past. Amazingly, my mind was focused and powerful. I was in tune with my surroundings. I was closer to God than I had ever dreamed I could be. Now I just had to deal with a body that was suffering from a stealth killer called cancer.

What was the cause? Was there one specific thing I could point to in my past and say, "Aha!" and know for certain that was the reason I had this cancer? Was it the chemicals I ingested? Was it the stress or the air that I breathed? The thought that this was my fault was a difficult one to accept. But the truth is that most of our physical and mental issues we have created ourselves, and somehow I would have to take responsibility for what had happened to me.

I thought back to the night I spent with the Indian ghosts. I had wondered if they had the power to heal me. I took the amulet I had found and held it tight in my hands. As I peered over the cliff where I was sitting, I saw four wolves tearing a deer carcass to pieces. I wondered if that would be what would happen to me, and if so, how perfect. Then I fell into one of those dreams.

This dream was not of the past or the future but seemed to be like another experience happening at the same time as the one I was living, as if I had more than one life going on at one time. I saw one life holding on to the other like it couldn't let go. Each existence was holding on to all the things in its realm. Then the meaning became clear. Let go of the cancer; let go of the pain; let go of the situation; let go of me.

I thought about life and how we hold on to everything with so much vigor. We just don't want to give up anything. We hold on to our problems; we hold on to stress; we hold on to our sicknesses. We hold on to lies about ourselves; we hold on to our past. If you want to live today, you have to let go of yesterday. Give up everything to have everything! Give up not being happy so you can be happy; give up not having money so you can have money. Give up fear so you can have peace.

God, as I sit here in this situation, I surrender my life to You. I let go of all things unto You. I give up this cancer. I give up this fear. I give up this hunger. I give up this pain. I give up the past and the future. I give up all that I am. I let go of this life. I hold on to nothing and nothing holds on to me. Thank you for Your guidance and truth.

The freedom I felt after that prayer was like nothing I had ever felt before. I was like a leaf on a branch, a pebble in the creek, the wind, and the water. I felt such power in this feeling of peace. Then all at once the sun was shining in all its magnificence, like it was just for me. The wind was blowing as if for me only. I could see the energy all around me. I could hear sounds of life. I was free—free to be alive, free to create, free to know love at the highest level. Surrendered . . .

I went back to camp and put the water to my lips; the water had a taste. I could taste the minerals in it, and I felt it slide down my throat into my stomach. I was thankful for the water. I took some of the hot rocks from the fire pit and laid them on my body. I could feel the heat and the life coming from the rocks into my body. I lay there knowing that I had the power to choose what my experience would be. It wasn't that I didn't have cancer but how I thought about the cancer. It wasn't that the elements wouldn't kill me; it was how I looked at them.

So it is with all of life. It's quite simple; it's what you think of any given situation. You have the power to choose how and what you think of anything, even miracles. Miracles are thoughts with so much intensity they change reality. Our reality is just what we decide it to be—happy, sad, rich, poor, healthy, and unhealthy. It sounds naïve; it sounds unrealistic. It sounds so new age. But it is just simply the truth.

The cancer did get worse. The pain and all the other symptoms got worse. There were times that I was delirious with agony. There were times I could barely drink water, but the difference was how I looked at it all. I did not own it, and it did not own me. I gave it no power, and it took no power from me. Physically, I was as bad as you can get. My skin was yellow, I had lost a lot of weight, and my intestines were not processing like they should. I could feel that I was getting close to the end.

Father, the end is near. I can feel it now. You created me, and now You will inherit me. I pray that nothing separates us now. I pray when I draw my last breath You will be there to greet me. I pray that You will allow my last days here to beautiful ones. I pray that with each heartbeat I get closer to You.

The next day as I walked down to the stream, everything seemed different. I no longer walked around looking over my shoulder as if to be attacked by something. I no longer feared what lay around the next corner. Nothing seemed as scary as before. It was if I was glowing and all things in the forest saw it. I did not struggle with the terrain but instead glided over it without effort. That should be how we experience life. We should move with intention, light and free, not constantly wondering what will trip us up or knock us down.

As I reached the creek and bent over to drink, I looked up in time to see my old friend, the bear, coming right at me. He was huge, bigger than I remembered. As he came toward me with the look of death in his eyes, I had no fear. In fact, I smiled at him. There was nothing he could do to me at this point. After all I had experienced, there was little left to fear. I was already dying, so it would just come a little quicker.

I stood up. I looked him right in the eyes and put my hand out and told him to stop. I felt no need to scream this statement or to be forceful. I did it with a deep breath and confidence. He stopped. He paced back and forth, growling from deep within, staring at me with his cold, black eyes, slapping and pawing at the ground. There was nothing I needed to say or do at that point. He began to look around as if he was embarrassed and did not know what to do. He then turned and walked away, looking back at me confused.

As I watched him walk away, I thought about what had just happened. And it came to me that, just like in this case, you have to face your issues and fears head on in life with confidence. Just look them square in the face and declare that you are bigger, that you will win. Each time you do that, you get stronger and more powerful. You become liberated from fear. You become the creator of your destiny.

I turned my attention back to the issue at hand, which was fishing. To my surprise, trout were everywhere. Had they been there all along, or were my eyes just clearer now? As I took the first one from the crystal clear water, I ate. There was no need to cook him. Every bite was incredible, and I was thankful. As I looked around, there were berries of all kinds, and I ate. I was thankful.

It started to rain, and I lay back to watch the drops fall from the sky. Millions of them fell from the heavens, and each appeared to have a mission, a purpose. I started thinking about each of us on this earth and about our mission and purpose. I had many conversations with friends about what our purpose here was, our calling. What were we supposed to do? My thoughts had always been that our purpose is what we choose it to be, what we want it to be. We spend a lifetime wondering if we will ever find it. I don't think we were born with a purpose. It is up to each of us to create it. I think we decide along the way; some choose not to have one at all. Others find theirs through certain circumstances as I have.

So there I lay, my mind and soul so clear. I had spent the last few months basically peeling my life apart like an onion, layer by layer and thought by thought. I had visited and explored every aspect of my life. I had seen things in dreams and experienced things that I didn't even know if they were real. With all my newly found clarity, my mind was strong. My spirit was as big as the universe. I felt like I was at the beginning of time, when there was nothing but what was truly real, the very essence of what we call life. I was transparent, and I felt like I was awakening to life after being asleep for a long time.

There was still just one problem that was all too real. The cancer was taking a toll on my body. It was not a pretty sight. The pain was so severe that at times all I could do was cry. My body was weak, and if not for the power in my mind, there would have been many times I would have laid down and given up.

I was where I needed to be spiritually. I was close to the point where if it was this very moment that I passed, I would welcome it. I had no more regrets, no more confusion, and no more guilt. I had forgiven myself for all the things that I had held on to. I had asked for forgiveness from those I had harmed. I knew myself on a very deep level. I felt God in every moment of my life, everywhere. There was no veil left between us. I no longer was afraid of what awaited me.

Week Twelve:

I DID THE RIGHT THING

I believe this is my twelfth week, although I am fairly certain I have lost total track of days and weeks. That's why I'm not writing the day down anymore. Today is. That's all I know.

That night after fishing and seeing my old friend, the bear, when I returned to the ledge, I looked around at what I had built for my shelter. I was proud of what my hands had created. This place was something very special, and I hoped that if someday someone else found it, they would receive all the blessings it had given to me. What will they think? How will they ever know what happened here? Maybe someone two thousand years from now will find it and think they discovered a caveman's dwelling.

I thought about my family, what they will learn from all of this. I know that in the end they will someday understand. It will not be easy for them, but in truth I know that the quality of their lives will end up better. There will be a time that they will forget and move on with only a memory of me. Just like when my mother died. The pain was unbearable, and it took everything I had just to keep going. After time, my life readjusted and day by day life went on. That is what life is about, letting go and living in the now. Life changes every moment, and those moments make us who we are; nothing stays the same.

I stared into the warm, blazing fire and thought about how many times in the last few weeks I had taken comfort in its beauty and life-giving heat. Not once did I take it for granted or not see the importance it played in my life. Just like the berries, fish, bugs, and the water that I drank. They all had a significant impact on my very existence. I'm not sure, but I believe that my diet had helped me deal with effects of the cancer, not to mention how struggling to survive the elements had kept my mind busy on living.

The last couple of weeks had been hard. If the cancer was not enough, I had to deal with starvation, drowning, bear attacks, badger attacks, and falling to my death. I was still here, and there was still life in me. The emotions welled up in me, and I cried.

I was delirious with pain and missing my wife and family. I started questioning my decision to live out my last days here. I was mad at myself and mad at this cancer.

With the little strength I had left, I picked up my walking stick and started wailing it around, smashing anything and everything in sight. I kicked at the fire, which threw burning sticks all over. I picked up rocks and threw them at everything, screaming at the top of my lungs and stumbling all around. *Why did this happen? Why do I have this cancer? Why can't I live?* I was a madman. I totally lost my mind. There was snot flying from my nose, and tears were running down my face. I ranted and raved for hours. I would fall down and cry only to get up again and start all over. Then from the very depths of my soul, I screamed one last thing: "I hate this cancer!"

There it was, the thing that had brought me here, the source of all this pain and hate, the very thing that I had not addressed in all of this madness. I had spent so much time dealing with surviving the elements and working through my life that I had spent very little time on the cancer itself.

I was mad. I was angry that somehow I had caused this myself, which was almost unbearable to think about, or even if I had inherited it. I did not want this cancer. I wanted to live. I wanted to be back with my family. I didn't want to die up here alone. Maybe Doug had made the right decision after all.

What could I do now? I couldn't just go back and check myself into the hospital, nor did I want to. What would that be like on my family? *Hey guys, I'm back. Thought I'd stop in and say hello before I die, which will probably be very soon.* I felt so confused, so powerless. Why was this happening? I can't pass from this life to the next in this condition; that's not why I'm here or why I thought I was here.

Here is the way it works. When you push yourself to grow, when you push yourself to find the truth, when you look at your life and question who and what you are, the old you will fight for its existence. Look at how many times I achieved a great peace and presence only to fall back to where I'm at. That's when you know you are in the right place doing the right thing, when all the old demons, wounds, and drama come back to pay you a visit. That's also when you have to fight the hardest, with all your might. Sometimes even go a little crazy. It's a major life decision, and you must make that decision on where you go from there and make a stance. Give up or keep pushing on. It's God saying, "You are doing a good job, but I must make you even stronger."

As I calmed down and starting thinking straight again, I thought about how we build up such strong feelings and emotions toward different things in our lives. These emotions have so much power in our lives and sometimes last a lifetime. They bleed over and affect other things in our lives without us even knowing it. Sometimes the struggle itself is not with the emotion or toward other things, it is with ourselves. The battle within can be worse than the battles the world presents to us. The reality is that nothing has power over us except us—that boss that seems to want you fired, the divorce that lingers on, the issues you have with your children. There I was, hundreds of miles from anybody or anything, and I was still battling with all those things. Wherever you are at, there you are.

That morning I decided to go back to the spot where I had found the Indian artifacts and spend the night with the Indian visions. I knew it would be a journey for me at this point, but I still had to find food, and something was urging me to go there.

As I started the trip, I remembered all the incredible moments I had had since I had been here, all the healing and understanding. How I saw things so differently. Now I had to summon that same feeling toward something so awful. The cancer. How would I do this? How could I see or feel any positive or good feelings toward something that was killing me?

As I looked around at my environment, I realized that even if I did not have the cancer that was killing me, if I was stuck in these mountains for long, they would have probably killed me as well. So should I hate the mountains and the animals that live here? I don't think so. For the same things that are challenging our lives are also giving us life. If I had not been diagnosed with cancer and ended up here, I would have never known life like I do now. So all of those things that we have had to battle with in our lives have given us life as well. With all that I know now, I could say that I truly understand what life is and what life is not.

Life is not hard, unless you say it is.

Life is beautiful, if you say it is.

Barely strong enough to walk and still hungry, I continued on. I found berries and grubs to eat. While coming up to a stream on a large rock overhang, I peered over to find a large varmint digging in the dirt. I wasn't sure what it was, but it looked like a cross between a rat and a possum. It could not see me looking from where I was, so it went about its business completely oblivious that it was on the menu. I had not had any meat in days, so no matter what it was, it looked like a big, fat steak at this moment. But I've learned since being here that just because you find a meal doesn't mean you get the meal. I don't know how many rabbits, squirrels, and various other meals have just disappeared in front of my eyes.

I took my walking stick and quickly tied several other smaller sticks to the end of it to make it bigger and sharper and to increase my odds. I closed my eyes and envisioned the throw and the stick. I looked up and said thank you for this meal that I needed so badly and made the throw. It was a perfect throw and silently did what it was intended to do. I stood there on my rock overlook watching the animal live its last moments. I would eat again.

I was not far from the Indian site, so I waited to eat until I reached it. As I walked up on the spot, I couldn't keep from noticing that the area still had a magical look to it. It was different than all of the other areas around it. The temperature was cooler, the trees looked different, and the ground looked alive. The last time I was there I was scared, lost, and cold. This time it was different. I was there to do something special, beyond anything that I had ever known or conceived. I felt it. I sensed it.

I built a fire and prepared my meal. I was hungry. I had found a beautiful amulet last time, so I started looking around while my dinner was cooking. I walked up to a small rock overhang and found what looked like a small cave. The entrance was blocked by some large rocks and bushes; obviously it had been deliberately hidden. Apprehensively I removed the debris and looked inside.

As my eyes adjusted to the dim light, I could see that there were beautiful clay pots and various tools that had not been broken or disturbed since they were left there. The pots were sealed up with some kind of sticky black tar and string. One in particular had some amazing inscriptions on it and looked different than the rest. Feeling like a grave robber, I took my knife and with some work pried it open. Immediately I was hit with an incredible smell of flowers, leaves, and roots. Everything was still moist like the day it was put in there. I took some out and tasted the mixture, and it was amazing. It had a sweet, powerful flavor that reminded me of honeysuckle with a kick. I took the mixture and the pot back down to the fire and added hot water to it to make a tea. The smell was intoxicating, and the rich aroma filled the air around me. This was a special mixture, so I sipped it with respect and admiration for its creator.

After eating and drinking my tea, I stared deep into the fire. I felt safe here, for some reason, and better just being here. Reaching down to the fire, I did something crazy but at the same time so fitting. I took one of the sticks from the fire with a glowing hot tip and stuck it to the inside of my forearm. The intense heat and smell of burning flesh was about all I could take, but I left it there. I screamed out to the top of my lungs and rocked back and forth. The pain was intense, but with each second I felt even more powerful. I was in the moment, my mind was clear, and I was focused. This brand on my arm was to signify my commitment to all the life that is front of me. After I removed the burning stick, I just smiled, as I saw it was in the shape of a cross.

I was there, where I needed to be mentally and emotionally for the prayers I would pray and for the love that I would give to this disease that was killing me.

God, I pray to You this day. I pray that You will guide me this night, show me what it is I am to do. My end is near, and I have little left to do. I have struggled with the reasons I'm here. I have struggled with what I have done to my family. I have survived the elements. I have cried and screamed. I have let go of everything in my life. I have examined every aspect of my life and taken responsibility. I have reached deep inside for understanding. My mind is clear, and my soul is beautiful. Come to me this night and express Yourself through me; reach down and touch me. Show me why I am here this night and what I am to do.

As I thought of how in love with life I was, I became so grateful for all of life. How can you be only thankful with what you perceive as the good things when all things are good? All things have a reason and a purpose whether you created them or not. If you could love and appreciate everything in your life, no matter how bad it seemed, how great life would be?

With the warmth of the fire at my feet and a full stomach, I went into a deep meditation. My body felt like it was filled with light. Everything around me seemed to move in half speed. I could feel the energy from the trees and rocks and ground. The sky fell on me like a warm blanket. I could feel the blood coursing through my veins. I could feel the air moving through my lungs. The hairs on my body were lit up with light. There was no other place on earth I would rather have been. This was one of the most special moments of my life. I couldn't feel the separation between my body and my spirit. I was one with everything, and everything was one with me. Love filled every cell in my body, and with every breath I felt even more love.

The trees lit up.

The ground shook with approval,

and the angels sang.

As I sat there in an enlightened, dreamy state, I was completely amazed watching all of the incredible things that were going on around me. Staring ahead, out of nowhere the same ripple in the air appeared before me just like the last time. And just like before, I could see right through it, yet it seemed to vibrate or shimmer. It was much bigger than the first one, and as it got closer, it got even bigger and intensified. And it started to change into different shapes. One by one the shapes magically manifested into Indians. The first two were my Indians from before, and then others came after them. There must have been at least twelve, all dressed in traditional garments and head dressings. Some began to dance around me while others laid their hands on me. All of them were chanting and looking up to the sky. The two from before blew smoke from a pipe onto my body.

Then, one by one, each started stepping aside. As they each cleared away, I looked up and saw one last one that had not been there before. But this one was dressed with the head of a monster. It looked half buffalo, half devil. It had large, gnashing teeth with mud and blood all over it. The eyes were those of a demon, glowing red with fire. All of the Indians stared at me with questioning expressions, like they were waiting for me to do something. In fear, I screamed out, "I hate you! Go away from me!" As I repeated it, it came closer and closer.

Then the old Indian said to me, "This is your brother; would you not love him? This is the thing you fear the most."

My heart sank. I knew what that meant somehow. I thought back to all the things I had learned, all the things that got me to this point in my journey. I thought about what I said about attacking your fears head on and allowing the fears from our past to dictate our actions of the day. I thought about all of the power I had discovered that I never knew I had and all that I had overcome since being here. I looked straight into the monster's glowing, red eyes and, with all the power I had, declared to him out loud, "I love you, my brother. You and I are one. I love you, my sins and my fears. I understand why you are here and what you are. I understand what I am to do because of you."

For a moment, he just stared back at me, pacing back and forth. We stared at each as though we were in a chess match. Both of us were trying to gain power over the other. Then I remembered the amulet hanging around my neck. I took it off and held it out to him. He stopped dead in his tracks. Then right in front of my eyes he started to change forms. It was incredible and unbelievable. Slowly and purposefully, he began changing from an ugly beast to a beautiful eagle. This eagle was six feet tall, wide as a car, and absolutely stunning. I continued to speak to him, holding my amulet high, speaking to his beauty, strength, and power. He then turned to me, looking me up and down, and the monster that had turned into an eagle stepped back and extended his great wings, flapping them as if testing them for the first time. With a great leap and a burst of power, he flew up into the sky and disappeared into the distance

The vision was clear to me. I had to address this cancer with something other than hate and fear. The more I feared it and hated it, the more powerful it became. The more I looked at it and saw it for what it was, the less power it had over me. Life is much like this. When we choose, unconsciously or not, to ignore the very things in our lives that scare us the most or present the greatest challenge, the more they gain control. We have all heard the saying that what you resist persists. What came to my mind right after the dream was *face your fears and be free.*

I lay there and thought of all the fears I had in my life and how much they controlled me, and I became almost sick. When we don't face the monsters in our lives, we are not truly free. Our actions and thoughts are dictated by what we fear the most. It's amazing how long we live with these monsters and allow them to affect our lives. To be free, you have to deal with life's issues. If you don't deal with the issues, then each move you make in life is based on the issues you haven't dealt with.

My dear Father, I am ready to face this demon that I have allowed to control my mind, my body, and my spirit. I pray that You will give me strength and courage to look at it straight on and do what I need to do. I pray that You will let me see it as it really is, not as I have made it out to be. Give me the power to do and become all that is possible.

For a long while, I stayed there building up my strength. I allowed all the fear of the cancer to surface because I did not want to leave any residue of that fear behind in my mind. The thoughts of fear were real, and I did not want to give them new roots to grow. I remembered reading once that the fear could kill you as quickly as the bullet. My fear of the cancer fed the cancer, and in that, fear held the balance of my life. As long as I fed the cancer with fear, it controlled me. When I released the fear and stopped nourishing the demon of death inside me, it no longer had control over my life.

I began to meditate, clearing my mind of all thoughts and even all my memories. I imagined my body like the water in the streams, transparent and clear. I felt the heat from the fire warming me. The energy from all the trees and rocks was coming into my body. How incredible our bodies are. What they do, how they work. We all take our marvelous existence for granted every day without giving credit to the phenomenal functioning machine that is our body. We spend more time marveling over how our iPod works than we do the true miracle of life, our bodies.

A great and all-encompassing new love for this body overwhelmed me. I felt truly blessed to have this body. I came to the point where remorse for my past actions, for the abuse I had inflicted on this perfect machine, my body, gave me great sorrow. Here I had the most precious thing in the world, and I had treated it like a pair of old shoes. Why do we do this? Wouldn't it make sense, considering all of all the possessions we have, to take care of this one with the most passion? It's more important than a job, a car, a relationship, or money. But we continue to spend more time and energy on all of these other things. How many people lying in hospitals, sick and dying, would give up all their money and possessions to have their bodies back strong and well?

I was totally fascinated at what my body was and how it was working, and as I pondered and appreciated this incredible organism, it seemed to respond. It was like I was looking into a microscope deep inside my body. Each organ that I focused on presented itself fully, intentionally. I started with my brain, then my eyes, and down to my heart. It was like looking at God in all of His glory. I could see all the veins carrying oxygen and nutrients to all the parts of my body. The body didn't need me to command it; it was thinking all by itself, knowing exactly what to do and when to do it, a perfect and complete world within itself.

Then I saw it, an area down by my liver. It was a dark mass with many outreaching fingers that attached themselves to different muscles and organs, stealing blood from wherever they could. The sight of this brought over me a great feeling of apprehension. As I focused on the mass, it seemed to sense my fear and gain strength. My first reaction was to ignore it and move on. But then it was said to me again, *Face your fears and be free. The power of you is at hand; the power of me is at hand.*

Remembering the Indian monster, I looked again at the mass that was attacking my body and spoke the words, "I love you. You no longer scare me. You have no power here any longer. If you must be here, then we will be here together. God has the power to turn all monsters into eagles, and it is with knowledge I choose . . ."

I decided to use my brain to do what it was designed to do, obey me. I told my brain to stop the blood flow to that mass. I told my body to begin to send chemicals to that area that would stop it from growing and eat it away. Then I saw something amazing—my brain working; it was sending signals to the affected area. The veins started sending blood with all the life-giving nutrients away from the mass. Then it sent millions of little particles all lit up with energy to the cancerous area. They surrounded the mass, attaching to it en masse, until I could no longer see it. My body was now thinking for itself. I had asked and given permission for my body to do whatever it was it needed to do.

I thought about life and how we just don't give ourselves permission to be what we want, to have what we want. Maybe it's because we live with fear; maybe it's because we were taught it's selfish to be happy or have what we want. The bottom line is we all need to do forgive ourselves for the mistakes we've made, for your mistakes do not define you. Then expect wonderful things in our lives by giving ourselves permission to receive them.

From this day forward I would give myself permission to be happy, to let go of the past, to forgive, to be healthy, to love deeper, to be loved, *to feel*, to heal and be healed, to be free, to be my highest self, to be powerful, to fly like an eagle, and to be loved by God.

God, I have not asked You to take away this cancer. I have felt guilt and shame for how I have treated this body and the things I have done in my life. The fear I have felt was the fear of asking for forgiveness and then not being forgiven. I pray now that You will give me another chance, that You will see in me the truth. I have had my priorities wrong. I have not appreciated what was most important in life. I have focused on everything but that. I am now aware of this and will become what I was meant to be. My body, my spirit, my life will now become the most important things to me. I thank You for all that I have. I am truly a blessed man. With what time I have left, I will cherish every moment and give myself permission to be all I can be. I love You. I love me. I love all things.

After my prayer, I dozed, and some hours later I woke, but I was not in the same place as when I started the meditation. I was sitting on top of a rock in the middle of the stream. My clothes were gone, and I had what looked like ash markings all over my body. There was mud on my feet and hands. Beneath me on the rock where I was sitting, there was a strange, dark, oily substance that had a strong, pungent odor. What had just happened?

I got up and walked through the cool stream back to the fire. My clothes were there, and the fire still had glowing embers. I drank some of the tea I had made earlier from the stuff that was in the Indian pot and got the fire going again. As I sat there thinking of what just happened and how beautiful it was, again I was overcome with just how powerful we are as humans. We only use a tiny fraction of the ability and power we possess. Our minds are cluttered with all of the trash we put into them every day. If we only used as much time learning and discovering the latent power we have as we do learning how to use the Internet or becoming an expert on sports, there is no telling what we could accomplish. How many of us really spend any time at all learning about the most powerful tool on the face of this earth, us? It is safe to say that very few even care. We spend billions of dollars every year researching how to fix the very problems that we create within ourselves.

My soul was different. My mind looked at things differently. The way I touched things was more deliberate. When I looked at a plant or a tree, I didn't look at it the same way as in the past. I didn't just see the exterior of it; I saw the totality. I saw it working, growing, breathing, and giving off the very oxygen I breathed. I looked at my body like I used to look at a Ferrari, with total awe. These bodies are truly a miracle. Our minds are truly the power of God.

My body was tingling. I felt light and filled with energy. I could feel all my organs as they did the job they were created for, each one of them with a purpose and each one of them working in unison with the other. When I reached down to check the burn I had inflicted upon myself earlier, it was no surprise to find it almost already healed. I just smiled.

I had struggled many times since I'd been there on whether or not I was doing the right thing, but is there really any such thing as the right or wrong thing to do? We just do. We create our own lives each day, and we are the only ones responsible for the outcome. Nobody else can determine our happiness or who we are. We own that responsibility of our happiness, our health, and our success. Most of us look for someone or something in the world to blame for our conditions. A friend, a psychologist friend, once told me that was called external locus of control. Blaming or giving control over to someone or something located outside of our lives. In reality, we have the ultimate power over our lives and what they are.

Moving forward with what days I have left, I will be at peace with the decision I made to come here. I will not doubt that decision ever again. I had experienced more and lived more in the last few months than I had my entire life. I do not regret being here, and I'm now sure that it was for the right reason.

The journey home was incredible. Everything was so alive and beaming with energy. I no longer felt like I was attached to this earth by my feet. It was more like I was moving through it. I didn't find myself struggling for my balance like before. Life is like that. When you no longer are burdened by fear, guilt, and anxiety, you realize how special your life is; you see things differently. You start to create your existence instead of it being created for you. You move with ease and purpose, fully aware of you and the others around you. You find the balance in your life.

I started to reach the bottom of the canyon when I heard a deep growl. As I turned my head, I saw three wolves staring right at me. They were huge and looked like the ones I had seen eating the deer that one day. I felt like one move on my part would be my last. They continued growling, showing their teeth, and the hair was standing straight up on their backs. This was a bad situation, and I knew they were not going to let me go. My heart was pumping, and my muscles were tense. There was no way to outrun them, and the nearest tree was too far.

As they started to separate and surround me, I picked up the biggest stick I could find and prepared for battle. I looked at each one and said to them, "You picked the wrong fight today. I am the greatest miracle on this earth, and you will find defeat."

The confidence I had and the strength of my spirit just came out. I sprang forward at the first wolf and delivered a smashing blow to the side of his head, knocking him down. As the other charged at me, I moved to the right, and he flew right by. But the third grabbed my arm and started pulling me down. I took my finger and pushed it through his eye, causing him to release his grip, and as he pawed at his eye, I kicked him right in the ribs. The one that had flown and tumbled past me was coming back, and I busted him with all my might in his mouth with my club. I was now moving with intent and purpose. Quietly, I moved with grace, to live. I continued to smash, kick, and stomp. With each powerful blow, they became a little more hesitant.

Everything stopped for the moment, and I calmed myself in a ready position. We all just stood there looking at each other, all of us bloody and tired. All at once I felt a strong, deep yell coming from down inside my body. When it reached my mouth, it had the power of a foghorn. My arms were straight up in the air, and my head was tilted back. I was the ruler of my destiny and my future, and I let the world know it. When I was finished, I looked around, and the wolves were gone.

I didn't know now how many times I had escaped death here, but what I learned was that whether in the city or in the mountains, there will be challenges in everyone's life. You cannot run far enough or hide well enough to escape them. But if your mind is clear and your life is right, you have more than enough ability to overcome any and all of them. Take on problems with confidence and the will to win, and you will win. Do not cower down.

I remembered when I used to visit with my friends, and a lot of our conversations were about our problems. We talked about problems with our wives, problems with our jobs, problems with our health. Each time we would meet it seemed like we discussed the same old problems over and over. This all means one thing: no one ever does anything about their problems; they just let them live on. In the environment in which I currently resided, that simply wouldn't work. If your problem is wolves trying to kill you, you must do something to get rid of the problem immediately. If you are starving, you must find food. It is very hard to be happy and productive if you continue to live with your problems. To be free and live with energy and passion, you have to take a stance, a stance on life and death, and fight the problems, issues, and dramas off!

As I journeyed back home, I walked with strength and confidence. I felt that nothing could defeat me. The peace of finally knowing in my heart that I made the right decision freed me. I no longer feared the cancer or hated the fact that I had it. I had peace and clarity and was ready for the moment I would take my last breath on this earth.

Maybe what I've done will help some people look at death a little differently. Maybe what I have done will make a difference in the way my family looks at their lives. Just by chance, maybe someone will see the truth in their own lives.

Back at Lazarus Ledge the fire roared. I got up and started dancing around it with animation. I felt free from everything. I danced a free, acrobatic, loving dance filled with emotion. The more I danced, the more I was filled with beauty. The stars were my audience, and the trees were my music. My body felt as limber as a rubber band. After hours of totally letting myself go, my body covered in sweat, I lay down and fell into the deepest sleep I had ever experienced. I dreamed so intently, so passionately. That night in my dream, I gave God my soul and devotion.

Week Fifteen:

MAKING PLANS

That morning when I awoke, I felt better than I had in my entire life, even with the cancer still invading my body. My mind was like a crystal ball. I could see all the things I summoned. Things that were happening around me, things I had done, things that had been done to me, the outcomes from decisions I had made, and the dramas I had created. Much like the dreams I'd had, they were as clear as if they were actually happening. I sat there and allowed each of the visions to come and reveal itself at my bidding.

One after another, visions of my life came to me. Some were issues I had not dealt with yet, and some were ones still yet to come. I spent time addressing each one of them, asking forgiveness when I needed to and forgiving myself when I needed to. I also forgave those in my life that needed to hear it. Once more it was a very powerful moment that set me free. Much of everything that I had done here came down to the release and absolution of what was but is not now. If there is but one word that will change your life quicker than any other, it is forgiveness. It is the one word that heals, sets free, creates, and transforms all in one breath. If we really choose to live life at the highest level, we must get rid of the guilt and forgive ourselves and forgive others. We have to give ourselves permission to be free, to be released.

There were visions of all the things I had done right. Many times I had encouraged, listened, and touched the people around me and never even knew it. Through words and touch I had created healing and love. I had created hope in times of despair. I had lifted up and inspired.

Many times I had made good decisions, and those had led me to beautiful moments in my life. There were times I was empathetic and caring. There were more of these than I remembered, and as I watched, I was able to see the positive impact I had on each person. I saw then the impact they had on others around them. I understood more than ever how connected we really are. So I watched each one knowing that there was a reason I was to experience them. As each one manifested, I felt a sense of importance, not self-importance, but the magnitude we each play in each other's lives and how important that is. If each of us only knew the impact we have on one another every day, we would be more deliberate with how we act and react. We would be more careful with one another's hearts.

Sometimes you have to push the pause button in life and get back in touch with your heart. So many of us have lost that ability to feel with our hearts, which is your soul and spirit. We have had so many hurts and so many times where we were deceived that we no longer trust what our hearts tell us. So we move through our lives just living in our minds. Then we lose the romance of life; we lose the excitement of wondering what will happen next because we've taken any chance of that happening out of the equation. It's better to live from the heart and truly have the connection to life and God than to live without it. That is where God speaks to us, and if you have lost touch with your heart, you have lost touch with the true essence of life, that place that allows us to see the truth. So if that is true, that means your heart knows the truth and you should listen to it. Careful listening to the mind; it has been programmed! The mind takes the accumulation of everything it has seen and been taught and then puts all that together to come up with an answer. The mind has no feeling or emotion; it's designed to execute commands. It's no mistake when someone asks you, "What does your heart say?" Unknowingly they are saying your heart knows the answer; trust it.

You must trust the process of life; you must trust yourself. It's hard to do when you don't believe in yourself. Begin with trust and end with trust. The alternative is to go through life not trusting anybody or anything, and that is a terrible way to live. I think it's one of the biggest issues when it comes to relationships. We just don't trust each other because we just don't trust ourselves.

I continued to take time to review all the good decisions I had made and all the good things I had done. Through this whole process, it had seemed like just the bad was coming out, but then again, that made sense. As I looked at each of the things I did right, I saw how empowered I was afterward. I saw all the positive effects that those things had on me and the people around me. There were many great moments in my life. The love and encouragement, the kind words I had said, the time I took to care about someone else. We are all good people. We all have so many good qualities. If you want to make someone better than they are, tell them how good they are.

There was one final question I had, one truth I still didn't have any real answers for. *Crystal ball, what happened to my marriage? What happens to so many marriages?*

The visions became very intense, and I tried to keep up with all that was pouring out. Did I really want to know the truth, and would I accept it? As I closed my eyes I saw and felt myself taking for granted the marriage to my wife. I saw myself not appreciating her individualism and what made her unique. I saw myself forgetting that she was more than just my partner. I saw myself working harder at my job than on our relationship. I saw myself projecting my fears and insecurities on her, resenting her for my own failures in my life. It was revealed that I no longer nurtured her journey in life. I no longer understood or cultivated her dreams.

Then I saw the beginning of our relationship when I was in awe of her, when I pursued her, when I was truly in love with her. I saw how beautiful it was to be with her. The way I acted then compared to six years later was significantly different. That was when I was the happiest, when she was the center of my universe and I was her knight in shining armor.

We had lost trust in one another. We no longer believed we were on the same team. That led to the separation of our hearts and our lives together. And in time, the communication stopped.

With her in mind, I knew how I really felt:

Oh you, the woman I desire. The one who captures my heart with the love that flows from her lips. She leaves me in awe and wonderment of her heart. She makes me want to fight for her and pursue her with all my might.

Oh, that moment when she is the stronger one, stronger than me, and covers me with light when it is dark.

Now she blushes at the thought of our encounter.

I have suffered much and been broken, down on my knees so that I could be ready for you.

I am ready. Where are you, my love?

I call out for our eyes to meet and ready myself for that first touch; my still beating heart waits steady.

I prepare myself—mind, body and soul. I know you hear me. I know you see me. I offer my strength to you.

I know your heart shudders and has fear of memories gone past. Put them behind you, for the days that will come will allow you, my beautiful flower, to blossom and reveal your true beauty.

No one else will do. All my heart has been saved for you. All else has been removed to make room for you.

All the battles have been fought, and I, the victor, will delight in the scars, for they were a small price to pay. There will be no greater moment than our encounter, than our lives together.

Even the harsh words will remind me of the greatness of our love and how God blesses me.

As I continued to look into my crystal ball, I saw one more important task I had to do. I saw that I was to make a trip back into town. I saw I was to write my wife and family a letter with a message. This was something that I had not considered. I had not thought about ever seeing another human again. I had wondered many times what it would be like to be back in society again. What would it be like to hear conversations, to have a conversation, to eat at a restaurant? It had been months since I had talked to anyone. Would I be able to carry on a conversation? What would I say? How would I act?

Along with the idea of being back in civilization came a lot of anxiety. How would people react to me? How would I react to people? Did I have the strength left to make it back? It didn't matter. None of those questions mattered because I had faith in the vision I had seen and I had unfinished business back in my old life. My family and friends deserved an explanation, and I was the only one who could give them that.

I had to start planning my trip back and start writing the letter that I would send to my wife. That was going to be hard.

I decided to leave in three days. There were still things I needed to do, and I wanted to take my time writing the letter. I would need to clean myself up the best I could. The last time I saw myself, my reflection at the lake, it was not a pretty sight. My beard had grown long, I had lost about thirty pounds, and all my clothes were a mess.

I spent the day working on some bracelets I had started and some carvings that were coming along. I worked on the drawings on the wall depicting my life here. As I looked around at my dwelling, I remembered at all the things that had happened here, so many revelations and dreams, so many prayers and tears. There were the incredible challenges just to stay alive, true, but this was a special place. This place gave me warmth and safety. I had been protected from the elements here. It had been the perfect place to do what I had to do. I hoped someday it would offer someone else in need the same it offered to me. Not a shrine, but a place to be resurrected, a place to find the truth.

Thinking back to the day I named this place Lazarus Ledge, it occurred to me that although I had not risen from the physical death, in one sense I actually had. The Lazarus phenomenon referred to a life that was restored by Jesus after resuscitation by every other earthly means had been suspended. It was at a time when no hope was left. My life had been given back to me. Hope had been given back, and much more. I could now see what life was meant to be. It was meant to be dynamic! It was meant to be, and is, magical, amazing, and abundant!

I still had to contend with the matter of finding food. Because my diet had improved so much with the healthy berries and nuts, I didn't need as much as I had in that other world. It was only once every three or four days that I would catch a rabbit or squirrel in one of my traps. But today was one of those lucky days, and for lunch I ate rabbit. For dessert, I had some wild blackberries that I cooked into a broth with added spices that I had found at the Indian site.

With a full stomach, I gathered myself and started the letter. I didn't know where to begin. Each time I started, I just couldn't put it into words. I prayed, *God, give me the wisdom and the ability to put into words what has happened here. Allow me to the best of my ability to convey what You have done to me. Help me to portray the truth, Your truth, Your message.*

Again I started back on the letter. It came to me that this was not a letter of hurt or pain; it was not a letter of shame or guilt. It was a letter of beauty, love, forginess, greatness, and hope. The whole process had been about finding truth and taking responsibility for my actions. From this my hopes and prayers would be that someone would find something out of all this and make changes in their lives.

To my wife, family, and friends,

I hope this letter finds you all happy and well. I know all of you must be worried so. I know that all of you must have cried much. Open your minds and hearts to receive the thoughts that will follow. I pray that as you read these words, God will give you the wisdom to feel with your souls that which can change your life. Please find a quiet space and take your time in reading this. I know how busy you all are, and I know the things consuming your minds. I only ask for these next few minutes that you clear your minds of all of the current worries and issues. I will be there with each of you on this journey.

I love each of you more than you could know. This love I feel is the love of the very essence of creation. I see each of you in my mind and feel your presence in my soul. You are each a miracle of life, capable of so much love and beauty, capable of so much compassion and passion. Your ability to heal and be healed has no equal. The stars lend you their energy to light up your lives. The very air that you breathe, your brother will breathe and know you, as you will know him.

Your love to each other is the Creator's way of you knowing Him. Never forget this. That love is more valuable than all the gold and silver left in the ground. Let it fill your hearts and minds and the hearts and minds of those in your life. I have experienced His love and His beauty. Know that it is there for you; ask and you will receive.

Take pleasure in the review of your life that will come. Do not fear it; taste the tears, embrace the emotions, for the outcome will be not unlike the metamorphosis of the butterfly. You must undertake this journey, lest be a diamond uncut. Make the decision as quickly as you can. Commit the time no matter what, and you will see every sunset, every dawn, and enjoy everything in between. You will dream dreams of life. You will begin to create a new life.

The path to peace, happiness, and clarity starts with the acknowledgment of what is the truth and taking responsibility of that truth, your actions. Remember what is important in this life, your health, love, peace, happiness, family, friends, your spirituality, the air you breathe, the food you eat. Give yourself permission to be what you want to be, feel how you want to feel, to live a magical, healthy, loving life.

Take care of your body. Treat it like the miracle it is. Spend time with it, love it, and care for it. Be thankful for everything you have; live your life with gratitude. Mend your relationships with others; ask forgiveness and forgive yourselves; rid your mind and soul of all guilt.

Push the pause button in life when you need to, and do it often. Get back in touch with your heart so you can hear your Creator speak to you. Never put a price on your heart. Let it live! Without your heart and soul, your life will become a series of operations.

Let go of yesterday, last week, and last year. The past has no bearing on your life at this moment, and, moving forward, you have the opportunity to recreate your life at any given moment. Have no fears in your life; they will rob you of your energy and life force. Take the time to be quiet and study yourself, who you are, what you are. See the good in all people. Only speak well about them. Your words are powerful.

Use your time appreciating others; give them value and worth. Spend your time correctly. Turn off the TV, and spend time in your mind and soul. Spend time with nature, your kids, your friends, reading, writing, and exercising. Take the family out in the country and stare up at the millions of stars and bask in the awesomeness of it all. When you are happy, look up; when you are not, look up.

Know at some time you will depart this life and move to the next. Make good decisions so that your departure will be blessed and beautiful. Know that this day in your life is more valuable than all the riches left behind. Get right in your heart, mind, and soul, and the things you desire will be within your grasp. Stop all the madness, drama, and gain power over your lives. You are capable of all these things and more. Please take careful consideration of who and what you are this moment and every moment there on. You are the author of your life. Take care in writing your script, and remember God is there to help you edit and rewrite your life story.

Do not be ruled by things of this world. Stop all the addictions you may have—addiction to chemicals, addiction to hurt and pain, addiction to suffering and drama. You are not a victim but the creator of your actions.

Listen to one another with intent and feeling. Trust one another and be trustworthy. Look at each other in the eyes, knowing that this is a gift that you give worth a king's ransom.

This journey that I have taken is one that was my destiny. I have chosen to become a child again, to be as the day I was born—no stains, no erasures, no regrets, no guilt, and no pain. I have chosen to be as close to God as my mind can understand with no veil between us. He has passed on a message to me to you. You do not have to go to the extreme that I have to be there with Him. You can be there now, go there, be in that place, just as you are, wherever you are.

If need be, choose to start your life over. Start over as many times as you need. It's okay. This is your life. Decide who you will be, what you want to be. Decide to spend the rest of your life with peace and clarity. Choose how you will now treat the people in your life. You have no idea how important they are. Choose to take care of yourself. Choose to live with passion and forgiveness. Spend your time focusing on the things that are important. End all struggles! Be thankful for this day, this hour, this moment you have!

I love you all and look forward to when we meet again.

I have gone on before you, and I am there now, and I wait.

Love yourself,

Allen

So there it was, my last communication to the people in my life. Just like that I had said good-bye. My hopes and dreams are that somehow some of those people will make changes in their lives and truly begin to live the lives they are capable of. My prayer would be to know that someone would benefit from what has happened to me. Maybe one of my friends will take it upon themselves to visit with people who are facing death and share my story, and that could be death of any kind. You can be dying and be as healthy as a horse. I'm not saying that everyone should pack up and go to the mountains to die, but create a sense of urgency to live.

I took the rest of the day to revisit my experience at the Indian camp and what I'd seen in my body. I went back there in my mind. I sent love and positive energy to the area that was infected with the cancer. I wasn't sure why I was doing this. Did I think that there was a chance it would go away? Was I looking for a miracle? I started praying again. *God, I thank You for my life. I thank You for this experience to get closer to You. You have given me the ability to see life in a completely different way. You have protected me and guided me on this journey. I don't know if it is too late for me, but if there is a chance, I pray that You will take this cancer from my body. In Jesus's name, amen.*

I was still hesitant to ask for an all-out miracle, but in my mind and in my heart I knew there was a chance. I also remembered the words that had been given to me, "miracles where thoughts that had so much power that they changed reality." Many times since being here I could have given up and just let it happen. But each one of those moments had exposed the will to live. I had screamed it out loud, prayed for it, and dreamed of it. I wanted to live so that I might somehow help others to live.

That night, as I lay down to sleep, I stared up at the stars, taking in the awesomeness of it all. I remembered what I had written about looking up and the power of those words. There was magic and mystery in the night sky, and looking up reminded me of what was looking down on me.

I lay there the entire night, becoming a part of all of it—the sounds, the temperature, and the energy. I wondered how I became so disconnected from it all in the first place. It seems that we all get disconnected these days, disconnected from each other, disconnected from our environment, disconnected from ourselves, and disconnected from life. At times, we don't feel like we belong, but we do, and the best way to get that back is to spend some time with nature. It doesn't take long to get the feeling that you are part of something much greater.

As the sun came up and shone into my eyes, I felt incredible. I watched the sun go down and come up and everything in between. How beautiful! This would be the day I would ready myself to go into town. I would need to put a bag together with some food and a change of clean clothes. I was a day's walk out of the mountains, and then, with any luck, I would catch a ride into town. I went down to the creek and washed and mended some clothes. There was no real chance of shaving, so I took my knife and trimmed up the best I could. No matter what I did, I was going to look bad.

While I was cleaning up and getting prepared, I started thinking about what a meal was going to be like that I didn't have to hunt down and kill. I could just imagine what food with seasoning was going to taste like. I lay back and listened to the sound of the stream like I had so many times. Staring up through the trees and feeling the wind blow across my face, I felt like this was truly the best of life. I slept for most of the afternoon.

That night I retrieved my personal belongings, like my wallet and watch, from a hole in the side of the wall that I had used to keep the mice out of my stuff. I had not looked at any of these things since I got there. I had mixed emotions. As I put my watch on and thumbed through my wallet, I remembered what my life used to be like; these things used to be who I was.

I got everything in my backpack and then sat back and thought about the trip. This place had been my home for months. I had some anxiety about leaving it, but I would be back in a couple of days to finish what I had started, maybe.

The night was alive as always, each creature on the same mission: food. Each creature was being a predator, and each was being preyed upon. It was a fine line out there. There was no discussion on the matter. It was simple survival. But it all worked perfectly. I remembered when I would see a dead carcass and feel sadness for the creature. It didn't take long after I got really hungry to understand the system. That was where I truly learned to focus. I had always had a problem focusing in my life. There were just too many things going on, too many things consuming my thoughts. What an experience to be laser focused, with calm and patience, totally in the moment.

As I dozed off to sleep, I smiled as I realized there was no more pain from the disease.

I was off on my journey before the sun came up. As I made my way back to the road some hours away, I thought about the day I arrived, my trek in. I remembered the anticipation, the fear, how my lungs burned with every step. I had no idea what it was going to be like. At that time, I had food and had no real issues. Everything was new and exciting, almost romantic.

Who was that man? What was that man? Where is he now? He is gone forever, only a memory. The man that stands here now is transformed, revived, and renewed. A man that now sees what life really is and all the possibilities. I don't look back in sorrow but look ahead with understanding that what will be will depend on what I choose to create, that I am truly the author of my life.

I made my way down and started thinking about Noah, the guy that gave me the ride to get to this place. I wondered if he ever told anybody about me. I wondered what he was doing, where he was at. There was something very special about him. Though he said very little, he said a lot. I never could forget that smile and the wink and the genuine caring I felt from him.

Thinking about that first day and everything that had happened since then made my knees weak. All at once I became very emotional. Tears flowed from my eyes, and the emotions from trying to stay alive and to prepare for death overcame me. I fell to my knees and wept.

My Father, thank You for this day. Thank You for my life. Thank You for this time. Thank You for my family. Thank You for all that you have revealed to me. Thank You for all the beauty around me. Thank You for my friends. Thank You for my body. Thank You for my soul. Thank You for my spirit. Thank You for all that You have given me. God, I pray to You this day. Fill me with Your presence, lift me up, and give me strength. God, express Yourself through me that I might be a light that shines for those who need You. Cleanse my mind and purify my body. Father, show me my path in life; make it so bright that I can't miss it. Guide me and protect me; lead me away from decisions that will keep me from living a happy, magical, abundant life. God, bring into my life those that will bring happiness and beauty with them. My Creator, help me to make a positive impact on those around me, that I might give back to life and leave it a little better. Cast Your mighty hand over the world, and help those that need You find you. Help them, my Father, to see the beauty You have created for us. I know You are with me now, as You have been with me all my life. My trust is in You, and my faith is in You. What awaits me is what You have brought me to, and I fear nothing with Your peace. I bow down on my knees and humble myself to You. Please reach down and touch me so that I might experience Your love. Father, I pray this moment for life ever after. Amen.

As I looked up to the sky, tears still running down my face and my heart totally exposed, I heard my lover, my Creator, my reason for life, speak to me from heaven above.

Allen, you now have the strength of a warrior, the words of a teacher, and the love of a mother. Accept your path, your truth, and your highest self. This is who you are. I am so proud of you. It took a lot of guts, faith, and belief in life to do what you have done. Move forward. Listen. Feel… and touch.

I rose from my knees and took the biggest breath of air I had ever taken. It was like I had been under water for an hour and finally made it to the top. I felt the air fill every cell in my body, and I was thankful. My life was uncluttered, my soul was free, and the truth was obvious! There was no more chasing happiness, reason, and understanding. I was now my highest self, in all my glory of self.

I made much better time than the trip up. My lungs and balance were strong and experienced, and I glided through the terrain. I kept looking back like I was leaving a friend forever. It now seemed like it was the only thing I had ever known. Would I ever see this place again?

I became very nervous as I arrived close to the highway. I stood and watched the cars on the highway pass by. I was not used to the noise and motion, and it bothered me. Was I ready to have a conversation? What would I say I was doing?

At first, the cars just sped by me. I really wasn't trying very hard to catch a ride. Walking was just fine for me, and if I had to, I would walk all the way. Then about thirty minutes later, an old pickup pulled over up in front of me. My heart was pounding, and I thought about turning around so as to not have this encounter.

As I leaned into the truck door, I saw a man who looked much like I did. He was a mountain man, much older, but physically strong; something about him was familiar. Without hesitation, he asked me what I was waiting for, to get in the truck. At first, we said nothing to each other. I just looked straight ahead. The sound of music on the radio was nice and brought back some good memories. As we drove down the road, I spoke my name to him; it seemed so insignificant.

"Jack's mine. You going anywhere in particular?" he asked, never taking his eyes off the road.

"Just the first town will do."

For a while it remained silent, and that was okay with me.

"How you been doing?" he questioned.

What kind of question is that? I wondered. He was acting like we were old friends. Wasn't it apparent how I had been doing? Something started to change, though, as we talked back and forth. I felt a great ease talking with him, and I started remembering all the thoughts I had had about taking the time to get to know somebody. I remembered who I was now, the new me. My life had changed forever—the way I thought, the way I felt, and the way I looked at the world around me. Soon I was just happy to be in his presence letting him know me and knowing him.

"Do you need help or anything? I mean, is there anything I can do?" he asked as we drove.

"No, sir, I am fine. I just need to mail a letter."

"They don't have mailboxes where you're from?" He grinned.

I just smiled and started thinking about what my mailbox had been for the last months. It was my thoughts, my dreams, my prayers; that was my way of communicating. I liked the old man. He was gruff, but at the same time, I could tell he had a genuinely caring nature and that he truly cared about people.

Timidly, I asked him how long he had lived here.

"All my life and all my other lives as well," he said. "There is no other place in the world I care to live. I've been all over the world and seen it all, but there is nothing like living a simple life with no worries or stress, no expectations from anybody; just live and let live."

Amen, I thought. I could hear it in his voice as well. There was something else too, something special. It was his eyes. It was as if they spoke for him; they were so powerful.

When we approached town, he asked if there was anywhere in particular he could drop me.

"Is there a restaurant in town that would let me in? I mean, I know I'm kind of dirty and all."

"Sure thing," he said, looking me up and down. "And they have the best steak in town."

He pulled over and let me out in front of a restaurant called the Cattle Guard. When I looked back at him, he just smiled and said, "I will see you on the other side, and we will have much to talk about. I hope you found what you were looking for, and Allen, I'm proud of you."

"Thanks." And he drove away. That's when it hit me. I remembered him. He was the guy at the first gas station I had stopped at, and he was the guy who parked my car, or at least I thought it was him. How could that be? What were the chances that I would see him again? Why was he up here? What was he? How did he know I was looking for something, and why was he proud of me?

I stood out in front of the restaurant on a gravel parking lot, in some little mountain town in the middle of nowhere. There was no one on the streets, and it was very quiet. I looked up to the stars above for comfort, and I took a minute again just to think about where I just came from and all that had happened there. It was a love story of a man, a disease, and God. It was a story of a full life circle, from death back to life. I closed my eyes and remembered.

There were several cars in the parking lot, for a town this small. That was probably a pretty good sign the food was good. I got my wallet out and checked my cash supply. Sixty-two dollars; that would be plenty. I was nervous but excited at the same time. When I opened the door, there were some stares and a few comments. I just looked straight down like some scared little kid and made my way back to the bathroom feeling the eyes upon me. What I saw in the mirror would have scared the devil himself; it was a complete shock. Was that really me? I did not even look like the same man, but there was something different. It was my eyes. As bad as the rest of me looked, my eyes were beaming; they were powerful; they had purpose; they spoke.

I washed up and put myself together the best I could. I went into the stall and smiled as I looked down at the toilet. Oh, the things we take for granted. As I stood there, I remembered all the things I had learned about myself and life. One thought that stuck out was that I was able to be myself without fear of what others thought about me.

We expend so much time and energy thinking and contemplating how we look and what others are thinking about us. That truth being they are probably using the same amount of energy and time wondering what you are thinking of them. Here we are, God's greatest miracles, all unique and wonderful in so many ways, each capable of so much. But yet, as we encounter each other, we all fear that we will be found out to be less than what we want to be viewed as. From that fear, we present ourselves in a way so that when people look at us, they don't see the real us. We are afraid that if they really know the truth they might not like us anymore, so the cycle continues. The truth is that all of us have had things happen that we are not proud of, all of us. Some just do a better job of hiding it.

I walked back into the restaurant and took a seat at a table by the window. Everything looked so busy. It was like sensory overload. I was so in tune with the energy around me that I had to consciously turn everything off. With my head down, I started praying.

God, thank You for this meal that I will have. God, we have so much to be thankful for. It is so easy to take it all for granted when there is so much. But not today or ever again.

Now I understand when I see other people blessing their food and being thankful. Who knows what their lives may have been like and the last time they ate a meal…like me.

For the last few months of my life, I had prayed without ceasing. It was a continuous conversation with God. There was no beginning or any end. It was all the time, from moment to moment. When I looked up, the waitress was standing over me with a less than welcoming look upon her face. She probably thought I had fallen asleep.

"Can I help you with something?" she said, probably thinking I didn't have any money and that I was most likely a bum or something. When I looked up, it was obvious she was looking for an answer, but I could not get the words to come out of my mouth. All I could think about was her words and how they felt.

As the words came out of her mouth, it was like they were carrying a message, a story. I was overcome with empathy and compassion. All in just a few seconds, I saw moments in her life in a smoky dream that I was accustomed to. I saw and felt what she was thinking and feeling. She had so much inside eating her up. She had an alcoholic husband at home who abused her. They were broke, and each moment of the day was miserable. Her kids had abandoned her because they could not stand to be around that situation. Her heart ached, her health was declining, and she didn't know what to do. She didn't have any hope, nor did she see a way out.

I shook that vision off and answered, "Yes, I would like a menu and a glass of wine, any kind will do." As she walked away, I shed a few tears. I couldn't believe that I was getting ready to order food. I thought back to all of the times that it took hours to find a meal if I found one at all. Now I was just sitting there getting ready to eat steak, salad, baked potato, and a glass of wine. This would be my last meal of this type, for when I returned home, my reality would be there waiting for me.

The waitress returned with the glass of wine, and, as our eyes met, I saw her. I felt most certain that she could see me as well, internally that is. For a moment, we just looked at each other, not knowing what to do.

"Thank you," I finally said. I stared at the glass of wine like an alcoholic taking his first drink after years of sobriety. How many dinners had I consumed, how many bottles of wine when they didn't mean anything? How many times had I complained when my steak was not exactly how I had ordered it?

Moments later she returned with the meal and asked, "Is there anything wrong with the wine?"

"No, I just want to savor this moment."

"Well, you let me know if you need anything else," she said, this time with a smile. Something had changed with her attitude.

Each bite was like an orgasm; every sensory button was going off at the same time. It was incredible. I took out the letter I'd written and put it on the table and continued with my meal. As I stared at the letter, I began missing my family so much I could hardly bear it. I wondered what they were doing at that exact moment. I knew that all I would have to do was pick up the telephone and they would come get me.

When the waitress came back to check on me, I asked if she would do me a favor and mail the letter.

"I will give you five dollars."

"Sure," she said. "It seems important to you."

"It is." More than you could know.

Then she looked at me and said, "Who are you? There is something about you that I can't understand, something that draws me close to you. Your eyes speak to me. Do we know each other?" Before I could open my mouth, I was spoken to in a now very familiar voice. *Listen, feel, then touch.*

"Yes. We all know each other, if we choose to. You feel like you know me because I have nothing to hide. I am transparent. You and I are more alike than you could know. We share the same struggles; we experience the same pains and hurts. We desire the same love and understanding. We want people to care about us, and we want to care about them. We want to be free. We want to be at peace," I said lovingly. She stared at me, and a tear ran down her face.

"If you know me, tell me why my life is the way it is. Tell me what I did to deserve all of this."

I looked her in the eyes and with power and conviction said, "You created your life with a series of decisions. Take joy in knowing that what and who you were yesterday is gone forever. You can choose right now what you want your life to be like; you can start over. Ask God to be with you and guide you, and then do these things: Forgive all who have wronged you, and forgive yourself for the wrong you committed. Forget yesterday, last week, last year; do not bring the past into today. Don't try to be someone you're not; be 100 percent of who you are. Let go of your guilt, let go of your pain, and let go of yourself. Remember what's important. Take care of your body and your spirit. Fill your mind with love. Make good decisions, and choose to create your reality every day. Spend tomorrow with God only. Choose what you want your new life to be; start over."

I took her hand in mine and told her that I loved her and cared about her.

For a minute, she stared down at the floor, tears dripping off her nose. Then she raised her head up and said, "Thank you, God. This morning I asked for answers today." She reached over and kissed me on the cheek and squeezed my hand.

I continued eating, thinking it wasn't quite what I thought it would be. After being on such a clean, healthy diet, the grease and the nonnatural ingredients overpowered the taste of the real food. My taste sensors were on fire, and at one point I wondered if I could even finish it. I missed the feeling of eating natural foods intended for my body to eat.

I finished my meal, which took me a while because my stomach had shrunk and there was so much food. I tried my best to enjoy it. My mind was reeling. What a journey I had been on, from the start to what would soon be the finish. It was almost not real. I looked around at the people and took in all the smells and activity. Even though these last weeks had been extremely hard and there were so many times that I thought I wanted to be back in civilization, I now only wanted to be back in the mountains at the ledge.

It was time for me to leave. I did not want to get too used to this. It would be too hard on me. I took out my cash and began to pay the twenty-six-dollar tab. I looked at the remainder of my cash and decided I would not need it again and gave her the rest. I kissed the money and laid it on the table, saying a prayer for her as I walked out the door.

I had a funny feeling as I contemplated my trip back. A lot of things were going through my mind. I thought about Lisa getting the letter. What would she do? How would she feel? Could all this have a happy ending?

As I walked out into the evening, I looked around at the town and then back up to the mountains. I thought about how much I loved life. I thought of all the great memories I had there. I thought about all the dreams and conversations I had experienced with God. Something big was happening to me at that very moment. It was as if life was showing me all of its secrets. God was touching me and showing me the future.

I walked to the street and started my way home. I was lit up like a Christmas tree. I could feel the energy of life pulsating through my veins, and there was a smile on my face as big as the ocean because I knew what was about to happen, what I was supposed to do. I knew my purpose.

The old man, Jack, pulled up in his truck and with a big, beautiful grin said, "Allen, are you ready? It's time to go. You have much to do. Your purpose awaits you."

Week Sixteen:

THE STORY IS TOLD

I had received the letter four days ago. It was addressed *To My Beautiful Wife*. The first letter I had read stated that sender had just met the man who asked her to mail this letter. It read:

> To whom it may concern:
>
> The man who asked me to mail this letter changed my life. I don't know who he was or what he was. But if you ever see him or talk to him, thank him for me. I am in awe of what is possible in my new life. With just a few short words of encouragement that truly came from a person who cared and the way he looked at me, my life has been recreated. I now know who I am and who I will become. I see the truth and live it. I hope and pray that he touches many more.

At that point, I knew that the person the sender was talking about could only be my husband, Allen. I could only wonder what the other letter might say. After getting through it, I had immediately packed my things and followed the map that Allen had included to get to where he had been for the last four months.

The hike in was much harder than I imagined. Going as hard as I could, it still took a full day. My lungs felt like they were going to burst. Almost every part of my body had cuts and scratches. I was so exhausted that when I when I arrived I fell down and went straight to sleep. That night I dreamed the most intense dreams I had ever dreamed. The dreams were not like any I had ever had. They were kind of misty or foggy. It was like I was there, but only as a bystander.

The dream was about people waking up out of dreams, dreams that were their lives. They were seeing life in a different way. They were communicating with each other; they were loving each other. They saw what was important and focused on it; they were letting go of the past and starting over. Some were spending time with themselves. Others were spending time with family and friends. In all cases, they were cleansing their souls and getting out of the illusion they had been trapped in.

When I woke, it was cool and crisp. I built a fire with the wood Allen had left behind and stared out at all the beauty that surrounded me. It was absolutely beautiful. Tears ran down my face, and my body shook with intense emotions. I didn't know what to think or feel. There was so much power here, so much energy, and so much love. I began to start the process I was here for.

The letter I received from Allen led me to this very special place. Also in that letter were these special instructions:

Upon arrival, build a fire.

Make a hot tea using the contents of the old Indian clay jar beside the fire pit.

Engulf yourself in the beauty all around you, and let it penetrate your soul.

Meditate on God's presence, for you are in a magical place.

Cleanse your mind of all things—guilt, hurt, pain, drama, fear.

Leave nothing behind in your mind and open your heart.

Let go of everything in your past so that you may prepare yourself for what's to come.

By the way, do you remember the story of Lazarus? That's the name of where you sit. When you get to the place you need to be, and you will know when you are there, reach up on the back wall in the crevice and pull out the very reason you are here.

I took my time, knowing that something magical and special was about to happen, and I did not want to miss one thing from Allen. The fire was warm, and the tea made from the strange concoction was incredible. As I did the things Allen asked, I started feeling close to him. My life, like most, has been consumed by something other than me, and it felt good just doing the simple things he asked. As I meditated on God's presence here, it became clear that there was a reason all of this was happening. My mind drifted in and out of reality, and after six hours of cleansing my mind and letting go of the past as Allen had asked, I did the next step. I reached up and pulled out a homemade leather-bound book. It was the journal I just read to you.

Reading Allen's journal was one of the hardest things I have ever done. There were times I had to put it down and just try to imagine what it must have been like. There were so many times the messages rang in my ears like a huge bell. I felt this was the truth that Allen had always struggled with, and in the end he had finally found it. He had reached the point where he was able to transcend past his very existence. His vision of God and what God meant to him was apparent in the words and experiences he talked about. There was so much clarity in his words. There was so much peace in his descriptions.

I know the pain and the fear he went through with the cancer must have been overwhelming. What he had to do to gain power over it was nothing short of miraculous. How can anybody have such strong convictions and be that brave to willingly follow a path or journey this hard?

I took breaks in between reading and looked at all the things Allen had made during his stay here. I put them on and felt their power and love. I could almost see him putting them together. I kept the fire going, never letting it die down. I made many more cups of the tea, resting and sleeping at times.

On my third day here, I decided to take a walk and view for myself what he had seen every day. There were remnants of his life here, there and about. I saw the traps he used to capture food and bones he used to make tools and such. As much as I didn't want to think about it, I wondered where he was, where he spent his last moment before passing to the next life. I wondered what it was like. Was he still in pain from the cancer? Was he scared? Or was he exactly where he wanted to be?

Walking around out here was very intimidating and scary. I know what happens out here, and being alone makes it even more worrisome. As I walked down to the stream, I saw where Allen had built fires and carved on sticks. I wonder how many times he sat here thinking about his life, thinking about his family. I lay down exactly where he had lain and fell into a deep sleep. Hours later, I woke to a mountain shower. I stared up to watch thousands of tiny raindrops fall from the sky as he had done, and I started praying.

God, I know You were with Allen while he was on his journey here, and I know You are with him now. I thank You for this moment and time You have allowed me to experience him. I pray, God, that he was where he needed to be when he went to You. Now please be with me, and help me achieve what I'm here for.

There is no doubt that he finished what he started out to do, and that was to find the answers he longed for, to see the truth about life, and be as close to God as possible. As I sat there by the warm fire and read and reread what he'd written, I could see his soul. I could see God shining his light down on Allen and cleansing him. I could see Allen praying to God with all his might. I could see Allen dissecting his life. As I stared into the fire like Allen must have done so many times, I started thinking about my own life. How would I go on, what would I become, what would I choose, and what decisions would I make?

I took one of the sticks from the fire and brought it to my arm as he had done. I would create a lasting memory that would bind us forever, a reminder of the knowledge he left for me, for us. As I took the burning stick to my arm, I cried with emotions, not pain, and I thought about the exact moment he did the same. I cried as I thought how it would be if I only had the chance to have him again. I would wrap him in my arms and never let go. I would tell him how sorry I was for the things I had done and did not do. I would spend the rest of my life gazing into his eyes and loving him. How could I have forgotten what he meant to me, how important our marriage was?

As I read the last pages of the manuscript, one last page fell out. It was folded and addressed to me. Tears were pouring from my eyes. For three days I had just read the story of how the son, the brother, and my husband had lived out his last days. Here was what it said:

My love,

I will be the air you breathe.

I will be the water you drink.

I will be the wind that blows across your face.

I will travel with you in your dreams,

And I will guide you in the day,

For I have not left you; I have joined you.

I know what love can do now, and I know what we are capable of.

I love you on a galactic level.

I love you with the intensity of God.

Your loving husband,

Allen

I grasped all the things around me and bawled from the depths of my soul. *God, tell me he did not die,* I pleaded. *Bring him back to me if only for a moment. I need him, I want him, and I love him. He has so much to share and teach the rest of us. Give me a chance to start over, start over with him.*

I knew I couldn't leave yet. I still had work to do on my life. I wanted to do what Allen did. I wanted to change my life. I wanted to start over. I wanted to know my true self and remove all the limiting thoughts that have left my life unfulfilled. So I made the decision to stay for a day or two, a week or two.

As I sat there rocking back and forth, trying to figure out what to do next, a calm and peace came over me. It was a beautiful love, like I had never felt before. It was wrapped around me like a blanket. I felt a brilliant energy penetrating my body. I had never felt so wonderful.

And then, walking up from behind me, Allen lifted me up, turned me around, wrapped his arms around me, and kissed me with a passion that buckled my knees. Looking into my eyes with a penetrating brilliance of love, illumination, and joy, he said, "We'll start over together, my love. I've missed you more than you can ever know."

e|LIVE

listen|imagine|view|experience

AUDIO BOOK DOWNLOAD INCLUDED WITH THIS BOOK!

In your hands you hold a complete digital entertainment package. In addition to the paper version, you receive a free download of the audio version of this book. Simply use the code listed below when visiting our website. Once downloaded to your computer, you can listen to the book through your computer's speakers, burn it to an audio CD or save the file to your portable music device (such as Apple's popular iPod) and listen on the go!

How to get your free audio book digital download:

1. Visit www.tatepublishing.com and click on the e|LIVE logo on the home page.
2. Enter the following coupon code:
   d8ae-a446-f65a-5c61-3f93-ae7a-ef25-78b0
3. Download the audio book from your e|LIVE digital locker and begin enjoying your new digital entertainment package today!